Respectful Relationships

Editor: Danielle Lobban

Volume 424

First published by Independence Educational Publishers

The Studio, High Green

Great Shelford

Cambridge CB22 5EG

England

© Independence 2023

Copyright

This book is sold subject to the condition that it shall not, by way of trade or otherwise, be lent, resold, hired out or otherwise circulated in any form of binding or cover other than that in which it is published without the publisher's prior consent.

Photocopy licence

The material in this book is protected by copyright. However, the purchaser is free to make multiple copies of particular articles for instructional purposes for immediate use within the purchasing institution. Making copies of the entire book is not permitted.

ISBN-13: 978 1 86168 884 2

Printed in Great Britain

Zenith Print Group

Acknowledgements

The publisher is grateful for permission to reproduce the material in this book. While every care has been taken to trace and acknowledge copyright, the publisher tenders its apology for any accidental infringement or where copyright has proved untraceable. The publisher would be pleased to come to a suitable arrangement in any such case with the rightful owner.

The material reproduced in **issues** books is provided as an educational resource only. The views, opinions and information contained within reprinted material in **issues** books do not necessarily represent those of Independence Educational Publishers and its employees.

Images

Cover image courtesy of iStock. All other images courtesy of Freepik, Pixabay and Unsplash.

Additional acknowledgements

With thanks to the Independence team: Shelley Baldry, Tracy Biram, Klaudia Sommer and Jackie Staines.

Danielle Lobban

Cambridge, May 2023

Contents

Chapter 1: Friendship

What makes a good friend?	1
Friendships: what they mean and why they're important	2
Are they really your friend? 15 signs that suggest otherwise	4
How to tell if your friend is really a frenemy	6
5 simple tips to make friends	8
How to make friends as an introvert	9
I'm young. They're old. Yet our friendship means the world to me	10
How to get over a friendship breakup	12
My friend has ditched me	13
And Just Like That: Why it's so hard to break up with a friend	14

Chapter 2: Dating

What's the psychology behind first love?	16
What is love?	17
How do you know when you're in love, not just infatuated? Five signs to spot	18
Healthy relationships	20
Relationship red flags	22
The healthy dating advice I wish I'd had as a young person…and still need in my 30s	24
Are you ready for sex?	25
Sex and the law	26
Sexting	28
What is consent?	30
Sex and consent	31
Teenage boys uncertain about navigating consent and sexual culture, finds new study	33
How do young men navigate consent in a post Me Too world?	34
How to break up with someone… nicely	36
Can you stay friends with your ex?	38

Further Reading/Useful Websites	42
Glossary	43
Index	44

Introduction

Respectful Relationships is Volume 424 in the **issues** series. The aim of the series is to offer current, diverse information about important issues in our world, from a UK perspective.

About Respectful Relationships

From friendships to relationships, it is important that we treat others with respect, and know how to respect and protect ourselves. This book looks at breakdowns in friendships, how to spot red flags in relationships, and consent.

Our sources

Titles in the **issues** series are designed to function as educational resource books, providing a balanced overview of a specific subject.

The information in our books is comprised of facts, articles and opinions from many different sources, including:

- Newspaper reports and opinion pieces
- Website factsheets
- Magazine and journal articles
- Statistics and surveys
- Government reports
- Literature from special interest groups.

A note on critical evaluation

Because the information reprinted here is from a number of different sources, readers should bear in mind the origin of the text and whether the source is likely to have a particular bias when presenting information (or when conducting their research). It is hoped that, as you read about the many aspects of the issues explored in this book, you will critically evaluate the information presented.

It is important that you decide whether you are being presented with facts or opinions. Does the writer give a biased or unbiased report? If an opinion is being expressed, do you agree with the writer? Is there potential bias to the 'facts' or statistics behind an article?

Activities

Throughout this book, you will find a selection of assignments and activities designed to help you engage with the articles you have been reading and to explore your own opinions. Some tasks will take longer than others and there is a mixture of design, writing and research-based activities that you can complete alone or in a group.

Further research

At the end of each article we have listed its source and a website that you can visit if you would like to conduct your own research. Please remember to critically evaluate any sources that you consult and consider whether the information you are viewing is accurate and unbiased.

Issues Online

The **issues** series of books is complemented by our online resource, issuesonline.co.uk

On the Issues Online website you will find a wealth of information, covering over 70 topics, to support the PSHE and RSE curriculum.

Why Issues Online?

Researching a topic? Issues Online is the best place to start for...

Librarians

Issues Online is an essential tool for librarians: feel confident you are signposting safe, reliable, user-friendly online resources to students and teaching staff alike. We provide multi-user concurrent access, so no waiting around for another student to finish with a resource. Issues Online also provides FREE downloadable posters for your shelf/wall/table displays.

Teachers

Issues Online is an ideal resource for lesson planning, inspiring lively debate in class and setting lessons and homework tasks.

Our accessible, engaging content helps deepen students' knowledge, promotes critical thinking and develops independent learning skills.

Issues Online saves precious preparation time. We wade through the wealth of material on the internet to filter the best quality, most relevant and up-to-date information you need to start exploring a topic.

Our carefully selected, balanced content presents an overview and insight into each topic from a variety of sources and viewpoints.

Students

Issues Online is designed to support your studies in a broad range of topics, particularly social issues relevant to young people today.

Thousands of articles, statistics and infographs instantly available to help you with research and assignments.

With 24/7 access using the powerful Algolia search system, you can find relevant information quickly, easily and safely anytime from your laptop, tablet or smartphone, in class or at home.

Visit issuesonline.co.uk to find out more!

Chapter 1: Friendship

What makes a good friend?

By Megan Bidmead

Since my primary school days, I've had many friends. Some of them I lost touch with as we changed and grew apart; others I held onto through the tough times and the good. Sometimes, though, I find myself asking: am I a good friend to others? Could I be better? And are my friends good to me?

Everyone has different friendship dynamics. For example, I have some friends that I know I can joke around and be silly with, and they won't be worried about it or think I'm strange. I have other friends that I know I can turn to if I need to tell them something important, or if I need their help in a crisis. Some are a mix of both. Depending on your personality, and the personality of your friends, the way you act and feel may vary.

However, there are a few great qualities in friendship that everyone should aim for. Not that we'll get it right all the time: we won't. Sometimes, we may take a joke too far. Or we might accidentally hurt each other. We can't be perfect all the time. But by thinking about these things, we can understand how we can be there for our friends: and we can figure out if they are good friends to us in return.

Be kind

'In a world where you can be anything, be kind' – Jennifer Dukes Lee

You may have read this quote before. I think kindness is underrated – and we need it now more than ever. A good friend is kind. I might joke around with my friends, even tease them (in a gentle way!), but at the end of the day, we are very kind to each other. Kindness can come in many different forms, but it comes down to being thoughtful and sincere. A hug when your friend is feeling sad, a listening ear if they need to vent, a reminder of their strengths and talents when they're feeling insecure – all of these small, everyday things make up a great friendship.

Be forgiving

As we mentioned earlier, nobody is perfect all the time. You're probably going to annoy your friends sometimes, and they'll probably annoy you in return. You might have the odd falling out, or the occasional row – that doesn't mean your friendship isn't valid (although you do need to watch out for toxic friendships. Sometimes people make mistakes – it's important to learn to forgive each other, to accept an apology and move on with a clean slate.

Be trustworthy

Have you ever had a friend betray a secret? I have – and I can tell you, it hurts very badly. There's something incredibly painful about being let down by someone you thought you could trust. If a friend tells you something in confidence, where appropriate, you should keep it to yourself. Having said that, it is important to realise when confidence needs to be broken for safety reasons. For example, if your friend tells you a secret and the secret makes you uncomfortable or worried, or you think someone might be in danger, you should talk to an adult you trust, like a parent or a teacher.

Trust is a foundational part of a healthy relationship. Without trust, the friendship will not last. Be the kind of friend a person can trust (and expect that of them in return).

Be honest

It's not always a good idea to say the first thing that pops into your brain, and it's important that we learn to be kind and tactful with our words. However, it is important to be honest with your friends.

Which would you rather have – a friend who would tell you if you had spinach stuck in your teeth, or a friend who would let you walk around like that all day? A true friend is honest with you – even if it's not always easy.

Be respectful

Your friends may occasionally do something that completely mystifies you. You might question their decisions, their taste, even their outfit choices. You might wonder how on earth they can enjoy the music they listen to, or why they spend all their spare time playing games, or reading, or sleeping, or something else that you don't enjoy as much as them. Life would be boring if we were all the same, right? It's fun to have friends that like different things than you – it's a great way to keep life interesting. Appreciate your friends for who they are, without pressuring them to change to fit in with you – and again, you should expect that in return from your friends, too.

Be a good communicator

Effective communication is one of the key foundations to all relationships. Being able to talk to each other and clearly say what you want and don't want is a key factor in a good friendship, as is the ability to listen to each other. Clear communication can make a huge difference to your friendships, and it's such an important skill to learn.

So, to sum up: kindness, forgiveness, trust, honesty, respect, and communication are some of the key things that are important in a friendship. Are there any other characteristics of a good friend that you can think of?

7 October 2019

The above information is reprinted with kind permission from Revealed Projects.
© 2023 Revealed Projects

www.revealedprojects.org.uk

Friendships: what they mean and why they're important

Lola Tulloch and Tulla Robinson explore their feelings about toxic friendships and what it means to have close friends.

By Lola Tulloch and Tulla Robinson

Confidants; supporters; defenders; motivators; companions; collaborators; energisers and thought provokers. Whoever they are, whatever they do, friends are important. So important in fact that, according to scientific reports in The Fader magazine, positive relationships can extend your life expectancy and reduce risk of heart problems.

Our best friends are supportive, kind, compassionate and caring.

It can sometimes be difficult to read another person when they're troubled; emotions are complex. It helps to empathise, put yourself in your friends' shoes, try to understand why they might have particular worries and concerns.

Doesn't it feel good when a friend provides comfort, without you having to say much? I know when I'm feeling difficult emotions it's not always easy to open up but the more I trust someone and feel safe, the easier I find it to talk. From past experience I know that my worries only get worse if I bottle them all up. Also, I think it helps others feel free to express their feelings when you open up.

It's healthy to be transparent and authentic with your friends so they know the true you. Even letting them know you don't feel good but you're struggling to explain it right now is a great start.

'The best friendships are healthy and rewarding relationships where you bring out the best in each other'

Whenever a friend seems unhappy, it's good to ask them why they feel sad, but you also need to give them space if they don't want to talk. You can still be there for them but let them breathe. Let them talk in their own time. Having patience and the capacity to listen are great qualities and can bring relief to a friend in turmoil.

The best friendships are healthy and rewarding relationships. You not only bring out the best in each other, but you also enjoy spending time together and appreciating one another's differences. When I'm with good friends I feel relaxed and comfortable and on an equal footing. When I come away, I feel energised and good about myself.

A while ago when I was really sad, three of my friends wrote me a letter. They each wrote a paragraph about how I made them feel comfortable and happy.

The letter made me realise how much my friends value me and take notice of the things I do. It made me feel loved. I think this was such a positive experience of friendship, through their caring and generous gestures I really started to feel happier.

However, it can be draining to be friends with someone who tries to control or manipulate you. At times like these it's especially important to see the difference between healthy and unhealthy friendships. If a friendship is unhealthy you might often feel sad, anxious or undermined in their company and be relieved once you're away from them.

'They tried to stop me making new friends and would get mad and jealous if I hung out with other people'

I once had a friend who would always ask to go through my phone, and would make me promise that I was their #1 best friend. They would want to 'phone swap' so they could go through my messages.

They wanted to look through my personal things like my photos and my notes too. When I told them that I didn't want to 'phone swap' they would get very annoyed at me.

It became clear that this friend had little respect for what I wanted and how I felt. They tried to stop me making new friends and would get mad and jealous if I hung out with other people. It started to dawn on me that this was a toxic and controlling friendship.

Luckily, I was able to drift away and started to surround myself with the people that I had a good time with and who really did care about me.

I think it's good to remember, controlling people don't have your best interests at heart. The relationship is based on their attempt to control you, not on mutual respect.

We have both been through toxic friendships and feel blessed right now to have each other and our other lovely friends. We encourage anyone who can relate to our encounters of negative friendships to make a stand and move away from these people. You can get more advice from Reachout.com.

It's good to be mindful of how people make you feel. It's so worth working out what's toxic and what's not so you can move forward with awareness into romantic relationships where there could be even more at stake. You can get more advice here from the Your Best Friend #FriendsCanTell campaign.

Thanks to SafeLives, which is operating the Your Best Friend Fund, for making this fantastic #FriendsCanTell campaign possible.

Mind Map

Create a mindmap of qualities that make a good friend.

Write

Write a letter to a friend to tell them how they make you happy, and how you value their friendship

Brainstorm

In pairs, think of things that can make a person a 'toxic' friend and make this into a list of toxic traits.

The above information is reprinted with kind permission from Exposure.
© 2023 Exposure Organisation Limited

www.exposure.org.uk

Are they really your friend?
15 signs that suggest otherwise

We've all had friendships that have ended up a little pear-shaped and it's unfortunate that most of the time, we all have to get burnt before we can spot a bad friend from a good one. We've pooled together our own experiences and come up with 15 of the most common signs that somebody isn't your friend for the right reasons.

If any of these apply to your friendships, we would encourage you to think twice about them and try to determine whether they are really a friend…

The 15 friendship signs

1. They only call when they want something

All friendships should be equal – which means that you should receive as much as you put in, it's all based on reciprocation and mutuality. If you're putting in more than you're getting out, you should think twice about what they are asking from you.

2. The conversation is never equal

Do you find that you just spend your whole time focused on them when you're hanging out? Yeah, that's not cool – we all have problems and things we'd like to talk to somebody about.

3. They put you down or make fun of you in front of others

A definite no-no. Usually, people do this because they feel bad about themselves and want to use somebody else as a distraction. Draw a line through any friendships like this immediately.

4. You feel bad about yourself when you've spent time with them

Sometimes it's difficult to analyse behaviour, but your emotions never lie. Friends should make you feel good, empowered and uplifted. If you leave them feeling like crap then you should probably re-evaluate the benefit you're getting from the friendship. Some people, unfortunately, just like to bring others down.

5. They are aggressively competitive

It's good to be a little competitive now and again, but like most things – you can have too much of a good thing. A friendship based on competitive behaviour is never healthy or a true friendship.

6. They aren't happy for you when good things happen

This is one of the most common tell-tale signs and it's also based on competitive behaviour. A true friend will want to see you succeed and be happy.

7. They bring drama into your life

It's usually the people who spend their time moaning about drama who are the ones causing it. You don't need that negativity around you.

8. They bitch about you behind your back

An absolute no-no. Friendships need to be based on mutual respect and trust. Don't put up with that crap.

9. Your relationship feels like it's built on conditionality

This is likewise for all relationships in your life. You should feel like they are unconditional and not based on you being or acting in a certain way.

10. Your friends bail on you

Sometimes it happens and that's fine, but if it's consistent then it obviously shows that your friend is unreliable and much less invested in the friendship than you are. Maybe it's your turn to bail on them, permanently.

11. They use your secrets against you and share them

This is malicious and absolutely nothing a true friend would ever do.

12. They are a bad influence and make you do things that get you into trouble

Nip this in the bud before you end up getting yourself into trouble. Friends don't make friends do bad things… or text when drunk, but we'll turn a blind eye to that one… for now.

13. They talk about their other friends behind their back

If they do this, the chances are, they do it to you too. It's fine to have a moan occasionally, but anything malicious would probably indicate that they aren't as genuine as they'd like you to believe.

> **Activity**
>
> Create a poster using the some of the 15 signs in this article that someone is not a true friend. Also include some signs of a good friendship.

14. They bail when you need them the most

So there are friends, who are, well… friends and there are friends who are still your friends at 3am on a wednesday morning in the midst of your breakdown. The latter are your friends for life and it's important to know that you can rely on a few select individuals to be by your side through thick and thin.

15. They exclude you from things with mutual friends

If it's on purpose and happening often, despite you bringing it up, then we suggest you create some distance. It is important to remember that sometimes it can happen accidentally so try and talk to them about it before jumping to conclusions.

It's not me, it's you: breaking up

Firstly, speak to somebody about it, make sure your response is rational. If it is, then deal with it, accept that it isn't your fault and mentally move on.

Once you've done this, you have 1 of 2 options:

Let the friendship naturally fade out

Stop making arrangements, stop replying and distance yourself from them. Eventually, you'll become increasingly distant until you're officially no longer friends on Facebook.

Or…

Confront them

There are 2 schools of thought surrounding this: confrontation can be good if you'd like to hopefully try to resolve things, but on the opposite end, confrontation can be incredibly empowering if you've felt particularly suppressed or upset by somebody. Arguments can be healthy, provided that they don't put anybody at risk and won't make situations worse. We'd recommend a mediator to help keep an argument balanced.

30 September 2022

The above information is reprinted with kind permission from Ditch the Label.
© 2023 Ditch the Label Youth Charity

www.ditchthelabel.org

How to tell if your friend is really a frenemy

She gives you back-handed insults and never misses an opportunity to sow insecurity and self-doubt in your mind, so how do you deal with a toxic frenemy?

By Christine Fieldhouse

Whenever Maya passes an exam, beats a personal best in a marathon or lands a contract for work, most of her friends and her family are delighted for her. They send congratulatory texts or suggest going out for a celebratory Indian meal.

All except Simone, who even though she lives in the same apartment block as Maya in Dubai Marina, and who showers her with public displays of affection, will always leave Maya felling less confident as if she's not worthy of any praise.

'She'll say well done but then she goes on about how lucky I am to have the time to train for marathons,' says Maya, 36. 'She jokes my son will start to think our nanny's his mother if I continue to go running every night after work, or to the gym at the weekend.

'When I passed my last exams, she hinted the pass mark was lower than usual, and that's why I'd done so well.

'But she says all this with a smile on her face so I get really confused and end up wondering if I'm being a bit paranoid. Then the next day, she'll text and suggest we have a spa day together because I was looking so tired and worn out.

'I don't understand why I feel so dejected and down on myself after spending time with a friend who's supposed to care about me.'

What Maya, a sales executive, doesn't realise is Simone, 38, isn't really a friend. Our true friends are kind, loyal and celebrate our triumphs, and are there for our lows and disappointments. They're with us in good times and bad and we know we can count on them.

Simone is actually Maya's frenemy. She pretends to have her best interests at heart, but she never misses a chance to get in a jibe, pass a sneaky comment and hurt her in a way that is so subtle it makes Maya question her own feelings.

According to experts, a frenemy will plant seeds of doubt in their friend's mind, then sit back and enjoy the fallout. She asks over and over where your teenage son was last night, then she tells you a story about how some teenagers were spotted smoking near the mall. She questions your husband's long work lunches, mentioning his attractive new colleague. With her raised eyebrow and a moment's knowing silence, she skilfully creates paranoia, self-doubt and suspicion when there weren't any originally.

Rachael Alexander, a counselling psychologist and author, believes most of us have a frenemy or two, but because the label is now on our radar, we mistakenly think it's acceptable behaviour and that we should tolerate it.

'It's impossible to have a friend who's also an enemy,' says Rachael, author of *You've Got This: A Student's Guide to Well-being at University and Beyond*. 'A friend is someone who stands by you and has your best interests at heart, while an enemy is on the opposite side.

'Frenemies are people who goad us into drinking and smoking when they know we've given up, or they bake us cakes when we're trying hard to lose weight. They raise an eyebrow when our children drop out of full-time education or take a year off to go travelling around Asia.

'They don't like it because our behaviour doesn't tally with what they believe we should be doing. We're also holding a mirror up to them. It could be they're afraid we're moving on and breaking away from them, while they're stuck in the same old habits and going nowhere.'

So how can we recognise a frenemy? Gill Hasson, a UK coach and writer, believes there are two types of these so-called friends and they behave differently depending on their personality.

'Sometimes a frenemy can be domineering and demanding,' says Gill. 'They're the ones who insist you go to theirs for dinner when you'd prefer to meet up at a restaurant. They're quite blunt. If they don't like your workmates, they tell you so. They like to keep control both of the situation, and of you.

'The other type of frenemy is passive aggressive and they undermine you by sabotaging your plans. They turn up late for concerts you got the tickets for. They give you back-handed compliments and say you're looking much better these days and they've been worried about you lately in case you were ill.

'At work a frenemy will take credit for your ideas. If she figures out your weakness, she'll put you on the spot and ask you about costings in front of your boss. If you're dieting, she will bring in cakes for the whole office so you have to say no in front of everyone.'

But why do they behave like this when, after all, they're supposed to be our friend? Experts say it's because frenemies aren't the super confident beings we imagine. On the contrary, they're usually insecure and jealous.

Gill explains: 'They maybe lack confidence and self-esteem and they don't feel good about their own self-worth, so by bringing you down, they make themselves feel better.

'In their mind, they think you're better than them, so they behave like this to bring you down to their level.'

But for how long can anyone put up with a frenemy pointing out to your superior that you're not on top form due to a relationship difficulty or a bereavement you told them about in confidence.

And just how are you supposed to react when they suddenly announce at a gathering: 'Have you lost weight? You really were starting to pile on the kilos.'

After all, trying to please a frenemy can be an exhausting process. They can be draining and you'll always wonder what mood they're going to be in.

Once you've realised a friend is actually a frenemy who is sapping your confidence and dragging you down, it's time to make the break. It's often hard to sever links if you have history – if they were bridesmaids at your wedding or they listened to you for months after your mum died.

'Let them go with love,' Rachael Alexander suggests. 'Remember the good times and, just as you would when a romantic relationship breaks up, move on.

'You could let the relationship die a natural death. Often, these things naturally fizzle out as we change and move on. Or you could have a honest conversation with them and let them know that you don't feel you're on the same page anymore.'

Most frenemies are well practised and so when we call them out on their back-handed compliments or their veiled criticism, they will try to convince you that the problem is you and not them.

'They accuse you of having no sense of humour or of taking things far too seriously,' says Gill, author of *The Confidence Pocket Book* and *How to Deal with Difficult People*. 'They tell you you're too sensitive and you can't take a joke.'

In this situation, Gill recommends we go with our feelings.

'See how you react when you get a text message from them, or their name pops up on your mobile,' says Gill. 'If you love being with them, you'll think: "Oh, great, we'll have a nice chat." Be aware of your first thought or your first physical feeling when you hear or see their name. If your heart sinks, your stomach turns over or you get tightness in your chest, it's clear there's a problem.

'Look in your diary. When you see you're due to have lunch with a good friend, you get excited and you look forward to it. But if you're seeing a frenemy, you'll dread it and experience some unpleasant physical symptoms like shoulder tension or nausea.'

Rachael says it's important to prioritise ourselves and make decisions based on what's good for us, not what's expected by our families or friendship group.

'If your frenemy gives you back-handed comments about not going to the gym or criticises your cooking, you don't have to spend weekends with them,' she says. 'It's about being your authentic self and respecting your own energy and time.'

But if your frenemy is a colleague and it isn't feasible to drop them from your life, Rachael suggests putting some boundaries in place.

'If you have a frenemy at work, make a list of the things you're not happy with,' she suggests. 'Look at whether they or you can change behaviour. If the answer is no, you might need to move departments or even jobs. Certainly limit the time you spend with them and don't take the relationship out of work.'

Gill acknowledges it isn't always easy to 'divorce' a frenemy, especially if they're a member of your family.

'If it's your sister-in-law or your uncle that's being a frenemy, you might still see them at family gatherings, so just limit the time you spend with them.'

And no matter who they are, it's important to look after yourself. 'Don't engage with them when they go into frenemy mode,' urges Gill. 'When they say you look a lot better than you did last week, don't ask them why they said that and why they thought you didn't look great. That way, you're not getting pulled into their game.

'Dealing with a frenemy is about self-protection. They can undermine your self-esteem and confidence and you don't need that. It's best to either stand up to them or disengage.'

Maya agrees. She now limits spending time with Simone to an hour a fortnight when she arranges to meet her for a coffee with other friends so she's never alone. 'I realised she wasn't good for me, and have slowly managed to cut down time I spend with her,' she says. 'I feel so much better and don't have to worry about being on my guard all the time. It's harsh but I'm happier spending time with real friends than someone who makes me feel bad. I plan to drop her altogether soon by spreading out the times we meet until I'm no longer on her radar – I don't have time in my life for a frenemy.'

Gill Hasson is a trainer and writer who is based in the UK. She is the author of How to be Assertive, Mindfulness, The Confidence Pocket Book and How to Deal with Difficult People www.gillhasson.co.uk

Rachael Alexander is a UK counselling psychologist and author of You've Got This: A Student's Guide to Well-being at University and Beyond. rachael-alexander.com

The above information is reprinted with kind permission from The Ethicalist.
© The Ethicalist 2023

www.theethicalist.com

5 simple tips to make friends

Making friends can be a little overwhelming and daunting for some people.

You have opportunities to make friends at every stage of your life, so being able to make friends easily is a helpful skill to develop. Hopefully these 5 simple tips will help you:

1. Just be yourself

You shouldn't have to change who you are to make friends; trying to be someone else all the time is exhausting! Just be yourself and let others see the real you.

A good friend will like you for who you are, and if they don't, then they are not the type of friend that you want to have.

Remember, if possible use open and friendly body language, like smiling, relaxing your shoulders and looking people in the eye, rather than hiding your face and looking down, as this will show others that you are friendly and approachable.

2. Be open to trying new things

Sometimes, meeting people can be difficult.

Trying new hobbies or interests that get you out and about, helping you meet new people. This could involve volunteering locally, or joining a club at school or outside of school.

3. Look for opportunities to talk to someone

Even simply saying 'hello' is a great way to start a conversation with someone.

You could also try conversation starters, such as giving a compliment. For example, 'I love your jacket, where's it from?'

Try and keep the conversation going by asking open questions (those which invite people to say more than just 'yes' or 'no') as this will help you find out a bit more about the other person.

4. Pursue common interests

From talking to someone, you may find out that you have similar interests or hobbies.

Using this can help build a friendship as you have something in common that you can discuss or do together.

5. Make the effort to stay in touch

Friendships take time and effort, but a good friendship will be worth the effort.

Showing willingness to stay in touch will help build upon the friendship. You can also use this to get to know them better or arrange to meet up and do something.

Take action

Remember: Making new friends can be difficult and sometimes results in rejection. When this happens, it doesn't mean that it's your fault or that you are a bad friend, it could simply be that that person was having a bad day or has different interests to you.

Don't let this put you off making new friends, even if you had a bad experience, as not everyone will be like this.

24 June 2020

The above information is reprinted with kind permission from the Health for Teens/NHS.
© Crown Copyright 2023
This information is licensed under the Open Government Licence v3.0
To view this licence, visit http://www.nationalarchives.gov.uk/doc/open-government-licence/

www.healthforteens.co.uk

How to make friends as an introvert

By Georgia Williamson

Do you consider yourself an introvert? Not sure if you are one? Introverts are people who feel more comfortable spending time with a few people rather than a big crowd and enjoy their own company too. They tend to be quiet and reserved, but not necessarily – sometimes it can just take them longer to recharge their social batteries.

While it doesn't have to mean that you're shy, it might mean that you find it hard to get to know people, or others find it hard to get to know you. Here are a few ways you can make friends as an introvert.

Embrace your hobbies and interests

Hobbies are always a good way to find new friends because you can meet people who are interested in the same things, and it can make conversation a lot easier too. If you have hobbies that you usually do alone like reading or running or creating art, try and find a way you can involve other people. Try finding a book club (they exist online as well as in-person), or a local running group or some art classes. There are communities of people out there who would love to share their interests with you!

Don't be afraid to try new things

Finding people who share your interests is a good place to start, but it's good to get out of your comfort zone sometimes. If you're struggling to find opportunities to connect with others through your hobbies, consider something new! Is there something that has always interested you, but you've never picked it up? Search for opportunities in your local area like a zumba class or a rambling group and give it a go.

But feel free to start small

Sometimes it can seem difficult to put yourself out there and get involved. If you want to try something new, or escape your comfort zone, but it feels too hard to try getting out there… then don't feel pressured to jump in at the deep end. If you don't want to go to a local event, why not try online groups that mean you can start making connections from home? If you want to go to a local event but you're nervous, just think about enjoying the activity and don't worry about the people just yet.

Reconnect with old friends

If making friends with completely new people is too much, consider people you already know. Have you fallen out of touch with any old friends that you would like to reconnect with? It can take some courage to make the first move and reach out, but it can be easier striking up a conversation with someone you are already familiar with – and that moment of success once you've reached out could push you to make the first move with other people too (new or not).

Look at the people already around you

If you already have a couple of good friends, look at the people around you who you might like to get to know better, for example their friends. You could have a lot in common with them if you got to know them. If you don't want to make the first move, your friends could make the introductions for you to get the hardest bit out of the way.

Be yourself

Like with any friendship, don't feel like you have to change yourself and your personality. You don't need to pretend to be someone else to make friends – the people who appreciate you for you are the kind of people you want to be friends with. Don't feel bad about turning down things that you don't feel comfortable with. If you don't want to go to a big event or you just don't feel like hanging out, then you don't have to.

Don't rush – it takes time

It can be hard putting yourself out there and getting to know new people. It might even seem awkward at first when you try to reach out to people – but know that it will become easier with time. Just give it a chance!

And remember – great friendships hardly ever happen overnight. It isn't likely that you'll make a new best friend right away – just like all friendships, it takes time to build genuine relationships, but all the effort and time you put in will be worth it in the end.

16 September 2022

The above information is reprinted with kind permission from Youth Employment UK.
© 2023 Youth Employment UK

www.youthemployment.org.uk

I'm young. They're old. Yet our friendship means the world to me

Intergenerational friendships can anchor a person in their local community, help them access new world views – and be fun.

By Erica Berry

Imagine someone living alone, loosely tethered to their community, with family far away. Maybe this person wouldn't say they are lonely – maybe they know how to muffle it, making cheery conversation in the grocery line – but the feeling is there, a moon tugging the tides of their days.

One day, a neighbour appears at their door. The two are decades apart and have shared pleasantries in passing, but nothing more. This time, the older neighbour holds a steaming bowl of soup. The occupant's first thought is dread. I am being pitied. Still, the soup is good. Literally and figuratively, a heart is warmed.

Who have you imagined for these roles? Who have you cast? It is hard, now, to see myself as that house's lonely inhabitant, having moved alone to Traverse City, Michigan, for a temporary teaching job when I was 27. I wore my loneliness like a rash, a secret under my sleeve as I walked my school's hallways. The presence of my long-distance boyfriend, friends and family felt spectral, like cheery ghosts who appeared every now and then from my iPhone. My loneliness swelled whenever I heard groups of people my age coming back from bars downtown.

If I thought I was too young to be lonely, I was wrong. A 2018 report by Cigna health insurance revealed that millennial and generation Z Americans feel lonelier than older generations; people who live alone do too. Statistically, I was perhaps an average lonely neighbour.

Doreen was about my mother's age, prone to doing yard chores in a sequined camouflage coat. When she appeared on my stoop with chilli made from an elk her husband had killed, I was mostly vegetarian. Still, touched by the offering of the sagging paper bowl swaddled in plastic-wrap, I ate it all. I hated to imagine her clocking how early my light went off on the weekends, but I soon learned to stop imagining her motives for care and meet her as a friend. What started as culinary trades – apple crisp from me, minestrone from her – grew into chatty updates. Sometimes I'd intend to go for a run but end up on the sidewalk for 15 minutes, my eyes watery with laughter as she mimed the Chippendales show she'd seen with her girlfriends at a nearby casino.

At the end of the school year, I gifted Doreen the leftover cans and bottles from my fridge, and she pulled me in for a last hug. Is it worth saying we are not in touch any more, that our connection was bounded by the proximity of our houses? The fact that our friendship did not transcend the street does not make it a failed one. Now, when I think of that year, I feel immense gratitude to those like Doreen who extended themselves to me, inviting me to kayak, to go to a jazz show, to come over for pizza or brunch, to join their writing group. Except for one, all the good friends I made that year were at least a few decades older than me, but because we enjoyed doing or talking about the same things, the age discrepancy felt essentially irrelevant. In chatting with millennial peers about my experience, I was surprised to see my emotional trajectory echoed. Not only did many of my friends who had moved to new places also feel shame about being a 'lonely twentysomething', they were surprised to see that in the absence of a 'built-in' pack of old school friends, their social lives bloomed vertically across the generations. In other words: the people who extended themselves to us young newcomers were often older.

This squares with the findings of Catherine Elliott O'Dare, a social work and social policy professor at Trinity College Dublin, who has found that intergenerational friendship can help root young people in new communities. O'Dare advocates for a conceptual mind shift, arguing for the 'insignificance of age homophily' and challenging cultural expectations that age is a good baseline for friendship.

'As one of my participants said, 'We don't wear our birthday cards around our necks,'' O'Dare told me. Her research shows that the engine oil of such bonds isn't pity or do-goodery, but the same things that fuel peer-age friendships: reciprocity, humour, shared interests. 'If you find a like-minded person – and that's a real gift in life – age doesn't matter,' she said. 'If anything, it can lend an extra dimension of interest to what is essentially an enjoyable relationship.'

When her study participants spoke about age in intergenerational friendships, they referred to it as a boon, a catalyst for conversation and skill-sharing, a door for accessing new parts of one's local community. A younger person might begin frequenting theatres or museums after visiting with an older friend, for example, while an older person might become reacquainted with a more childlike view of the world. Being with people of different ages helps us access new planes of both world and self.

I thought of Doreen's nextdoor camaraderie a few weeks ago, after throwing an inaugural party in a new house. During the pandemic, I had moved back to my Portland, Oregon, home town, settling last spring in a new neighbourhood. Though my community spanned generations, that night I decided to invite primarily thirtysomethings, thus subscribing to just the sort of assumption O'Dare's work challenged: that those in the same age bracket will have the most in common.

While setting up a food and drink table in my backyard, I saw my older neighbour walking down the alley. Without a child or dog to instigate interaction, my relationships with others on the street had emerged slowly, if at all. Only after bonding over street construction did I learn that this neighbour had lived here for decades, now alone in a house much bigger than mine. Meeting him with a wave, I told him I had invited some friends over to eat, and that he should let me know if the noise bothered him. He shook his head, grinning at the absurdity of the idea, then told me to have a lovely time. 'You should come by!' I said, on a sudden whim. 'I have lots of food.' He laughed, tipping his head with consideration. 'I'll think about it.'

I had forgotten about my invite when, just after dark, he appeared in the glow of the firepit. Handing my neighbor an ice-cream bar, I began introducing him to my younger friends. A few hours later, he found me to say goodbye. 'I had such a good time,' he said. 'I really needed that.' I told him I was honored he had joined, then watched as his small form retreated toward his dark house. The next day, he called to ask if he could help clean up. Everything was done, but I told him how much it had meant that he had come, suggesting we have dinner when I returned from a trip, and make it a regular thing. 'Name a date and I'll be there!' he said.

He wasn't the only one who had enjoyed hanging out. Over the course of the day, I got multiple texts from friends along the lines of: Thanks for the party! Your neighbour is the best!

I was happy the invitation had brought him joy, but my thrill did not come from being virtuous. It came from kindling mutual connection. How wrong I had been to assume he would not enjoy himself in a millennial crowd, and vice versa! How nearsighted it was, to assume we knew what would bring another joy.

In 2021, the United Nations and World Health Organization issued a landmark global report on ageism. It's a call-to-arms about a problem that costs society billions of dollars, shortens lifespans and worsens physical and mental health, increases financial insecurity, and exacerbates discrimination for those already facing ableism, sexism and racism.

The infrastructure of western culture – with its institutionalization of school, career and social life – has created generational silos, what the Norwegian sociologist GO Hagestad calls 'vertically deprived' communities. Because older and younger populations are often depicted as pitted against one another, competing for government support, Hagestad suggests that thinking of these two populations as 'book-end generations' may underscore commonalities and seed connection.

Though I write this as a 31-year-old, ever closer to the middle of the bookshelf, generation-wise, the value I now put on intergenerational friendships was cemented during those youthful windows when I myself felt most adrift.

The week before hosting my backyard party, I spent 24 hours in Cambridge, Massachusetts, visiting Elise, the grandmother of a high school friend. Aware of how few ties I had on the east coast, my friend's father had introduced me to her when I moved cross-country for college.

'I have to confess my first reaction was, "Oh, well, now I'm going to be a hotel or whatever",' Elise told me, laughing, when I called to ask if we could chat about our friendship. Her confession of past-tense apprehension tickled me: it was just the sort of honesty and no-nonsense humour that had first drawn me to her. 'Looking back on it,' she said, 'it seems to me we just hit it off. We went to a museum or had a meal or something. The connection was wonderful, kind of special from the very beginning.'

What began as generosity – her offer of a guest room when my plane got in late – quickly became a proper friendship. Over Lillet spritzes or mugs of lemon ginger tea, we'd talk about places we dreamed of visiting, the social currents of our lives, the things we had read in classes, me as college student, her as auditor. 'I just sort of kept thinking, "Gee, this is such a young person, why would you possibly want to spend time with me?"' Elise said. I had often felt the same way, self-conscious of being a couch-surfing slouch, even as I sensed our conversations unspooling with a vulnerability and openness I had previously known mostly with generational peers.

Research has shown that trust can be deeper between non-kin intergenerational friends. With different primary social groups, people may be less worried about their own secrets being shared; gone too is the envy and competition that can bloom among those on the same steps of the life ladder.

One winter I got snowed in, so Elise showed me how to make yogurt on the stove, and I walked her dog on the icy street. Older adults are often depicted as 'givers' of wisdom to younger 'receivers', or as 'passive benefactors' requiring care, write O'Dare and Finnish researcher Riikka Korkiamäki, but the language of pleasure and reciprocity – of a friendship rooted in the give-and-take of aid and advice, but also of jokes – offers an alternative for conceptualizing intergenerational bonds. 'The whole premise of friendship is that it's chosen. There's an element of reciprocity, but there's no "poor anybody",' O'Dare told me. 'Isn't that what friendships are about? That everyone is equal?'

After graduating and moving away, I began planning trips just to see Elise, aware I was now closer to her than the grandson who had been our link. I introduced her to college friends, to my sister, to boyfriends – what she called my 'coterie' – and over time I became familiar with her friends and neighbours, too.

A week after leaving her apartment, and a few days after my own backyard party, I walked over to my neighbour's big house and rang the bell. It was a warm, sunny autumn afternoon, and I was bored. I wanted to procrastinate email by eating an ice-cream bar. Elise was always willing to swerve our plans for a good sweet, and I loved that spontaneity, the let's-get-in-the-car-and-get-a-pastry attitude. Clocking how many ice-creams remained in my freezer after the party, I decided to see if my neighbour would help me eat them. After laughing at the sight of me, holding a dripping Häagen-Dazs bar on his stoop, he cracked open a package.

For a few minutes we stood in the sun, chuckling about the rat-like behaviour of the local squirrels, then, when the ice-creams were gone, we said our goodbyes. Walking the few steps home, I grinned. It wasn't because I'd done something nice – it was because I'd done something fun.

23 November 2023

The above information is reprinted with kind permission from *The Guardian*.
© 2023 Guardian News and Media Limited

www.theguardian.com

How to get over a friendship breakup

It's fair to say that all breakups, no matter their nature, are painful to some extent. You might be mourning the relationship, who you were in it or what it cost to get out of it. The ending of something we held dear naturally sears with the sting of change, even when we know it's for the best. Usually, with romantic relationships, there are familiar and culturally prescribed relationship beats we follow: we ideally define the relationship through conversation or physical touch and end it the same way.

With platonic relationships, we're rarely afforded the formality of clear relationship stages. It's relatively normalised to just bumble along in friendships without the same degree of intentionality we dedicate to romantic connections. Nevertheless, the degrees of intimacy cut just as deep with our friends so that when they are lost to us, the grief can be all-consuming. Friends are our chosen family, the people we form bonds with based on our personalities, shared experiences and interests. They are, in many ways, the people who shape our present and thus their importance cannot be understated.

If we don't have the relatively familiar, if flawed, crutches to support us when navigating their ebbs and flows, the grief is compounded by another sense of loss. When a friend exits our lives, whether it be through conflict or a slow drifting apart, we're less versed in how to deal with it. So, what can we do when navigating these breakups?

Validate your own feelings.

Admit to yourself that this is what you're going through and that it's a normal part of relating to other humans. Sitting with our feelings can be deeply uncomfortable, but not life-threatening in and of itself. Care for your suffering. Take your time to mourn, journal and speak to other friends about your feelings. Try to relay your own experience, dropping the storyline of who said what and when. What are you left with? How can you, and other people around you, support you in that?

Ask yourself what the situation is teaching you.

Endings bring new light to relationships. They can inform us of how we want to feel in a relationship moving forward or what we need to learn. Through this growth, we can move towards the friendships we desire, the kinds of connections that feed our souls. There are many different kinds of friendships — ones that survive anything, ones that reconnect after gaps apart, toxic ones, ones that don't weather changes, ones that nurture us and ones that simply are good fun. Figure out what you need and what steps you can take towards your desires. If you recognise your role in how the relationship ended, coming to terms with your mistakes means extending yourself the grace to do better next time.

Accept that life takes us on different, sometimes diverging, paths.

Sometimes, the biggest struggle of breakups is adjusting our expectations of what we thought the relationship was. People we imagined to be in our lives forever aren't, throwing our worlds into an emotional free fall. Friendships are subject to external influences that we sometimes have no control over. Life stages like having children, moving away or simply forgetting to reply to texts can mean that people drop out of our social circles without it being anyone's fault.

Luckily, your life and purpose exist beyond the connections you have with other people. Give your time and energy to understanding what that purpose is, even if it's simply to take the next breath. Excavate what brings you joy and pour your energy into it. Bring it back to the fundamentals of what makes you tick. Whether that be hobbies, taking a long bath or cooking a meal for yourself, provide yourself with pleasurable sensory experiences to soothe your heart.

Nurture the relationships you still have in your life.

Finding sources of support as you move through this experience is crucial. Make sure you check in with your remaining friends and ask for honest feedback when you're ready to hear it. Putting a smile on someone else's face can also jolt us out of the anxious spiral that's easy to get swept up in when we go through painful changes.

More than anything, remember that by observing your emotions you will witness them change. The acute pain after a breakup doesn't last forever, no matter how cliché it might feel in the moment. This too shall end. Not every experience is inherently fruitful — some things just suck. However, you are never alone in your feelings.

The above information is reprinted with kind permission from Relate.
© 2023 Relate

www.relate.org.uk

My friend has ditched me

By Sian Dolan

Being ghosted, ignored, or left out? It hurts…

If you've experienced losing a friend, you'll know how upsetting it can be. Friendships can break up for all sorts of reasons, but it can be especially difficult and confusing if someone who you considered a close friend goes off with someone else, stops replying to your texts or quietly 'ditches' for you for no apparent reason.

Growing apart…

We all change as we grow up and sometimes this can cause people to drift apart. This often happens when people make the shift from primary to secondary school – friends might want to go in different directions as they develop different interests or meet new people who they might feel they have more in common with. You might feel sad and find it difficult to accept that your friendship has come to a 'natural end'. Talk to your other friends or family to get support and try to focus on the existing positive relationships you have in your life.

My friend ghosted me

Being ghosted can be hurtful and confusing. Suddenly, your mate is ignoring your texts, walking past you in the school hallway and avoiding eye contact. You may have an idea why your friend has stopped talking to you or you might have absolutely no clue what's going on. So what do you do?

Well, you can try asking your friend 'what's wrong?' straight out, face-to-face. Tell them how much the situation is worrying you and let them know that you want to get to the bottom of the issue. If it's something you can work out together; great. If not, you might want to take some time to think things over.

If your friend refuses to communicate with you then sadly there's not much you can do. It can be hard to accept the end of a friendship but, once you do, you can finally move on. Try these tips to help you get over a ghosting:

- Let yourself feel sad and have a cry if you need to. Tell yourself that this is going to hurt for a little while but that it will get better in time.
- Be kind to yourself. You're going through a tough time and it's OK to have bad days.
- Talk to a friend or family member to get support. It can help to talk over your frustrations about how your friendship ended in such an upsetting way – good, supportive people can validate your feelings and help you deal with your hurt.
- Don't let this bad experience put you off making new friends. You have a lot to offer the world and it would be a shame if you didn't share your amazing self with new people.

My friend ditched me for new friends…

Sometimes, a friend might 'go off' with another friend or group. They may stop talking to you altogether and cancel plans/ignore your texts/avoid you in person, leaving you feeling lonely and hurt. It's not nice to deliberately isolate a person and it's not acceptable for anyone to say or do something that makes you feel bad. It can help to talk to someone you trust about how you're feeling – a friend, family member, or a teacher at school.

How to respond to someone who ditched you

When a friend ditches you for another friendship group, sometimes this can lead to bullying. Sniggering when you walk past, sending nasty messages, ignoring you when you speak… these are all forms of bullying and that's never OK. If you feel harassed, targeted, or intimidated by an ex-friend, please report it.

Watching someone you once trusted turn from friend to foe can feel like a betrayal of your trust. You might be worried about your ex-friend spilling your secrets or telling people your most private thoughts and feelings. If this does happen, this is also a form of bullying and it's a good idea to tell someone about it to get advice and support.

Moving on…

Losing a friend can have a big impact on our lives. Friends share our happiest and saddest moments and help us to deal with problems and situations that arise in our day-to-day lives. That's why not having a friend by your side can leave you feeling desperately alone. When you lose your 'sidekick', it can feel like your world has been turned upside-down.

It's important to get support and help from others if you're feeling very sad. Lean on friends and family to help you through. The Hidden Strength app can be a great supportive tool for you, too – use the Chat function to talk to our community or write down how you're feeling in My Journal.

Dealing with the break-up of a friendship is hard but it can also be a good opportunity to make new friends or to build a stronger relationship with your other friends. Spend time with those closest to you or try a new hobby or group to make new mates.

The above information is reprinted with kind permission from Hidden Strength.
© 2023 Hidden Strength

www.hiddenstrength.com

And Just Like That: Why it's so hard to break up with a friend

Olivia Petter examines why it's so painful to break up with a friend.

Ever since it was announced that a *Sex and the City* reboot would be going ahead without one of its leading characters, fans have speculated as to how the writers would explain her absence.

Kim Cattrall has made no secret about her, shall we say, lack of interest in taking part in any kind of SATC reboot.

As a result, the famous foursome has reunited for *And Just Like That* without one of its members, Samantha Jones – and now we finally know how the writers have explained her absence.

In the first episode of the HBO show, which is airing on Sky Comedy and NOW TV in the UK, Carrie Bradshaw (played by Sarah Jessica Parker) explains that she and the PR executive fell out after she severed their professional relationship – Samantha was Carrie's publicist – due to the way the book market had changed.

Now, Samantha is living and working in London. And we're led to believe that their friendship has fallen by the wayside, because whenever Carrie, Miranda (Cynthia Nixon), or Charlotte (Kristin Davis), text her, she simply doesn't reply.

So severe was the fallout that even when Carrie's husband – spoiler! – Big (played by Chris Noth), dies from a sudden heart attack, Samantha doesn't fly over for the funeral, nor does she bother to reply to Carrie's texts. She does send flowers, though.

What happened between Carrie and Samantha is an experience that will be familiar to many. Known as a 'friendship breakup', it occurs when two friends actively choose to part ways. And they tend to be fairly sudden.

'Friendship breakups are more painful than the slow distancing of a once close friendship,' says senior therapist Sally Baker. 'They tend to happen because of a dramatic misunderstanding or from a final-straw scenario when several disappointments, last-minute changes of plans or other ways someone feels less important to you drive someone to end their friendship.'

> **'Friendships breakups often happen during major life transition'**
> – Sally Baker, senior therapist

They're particularly common, too, especially as we move through our 20s, 30s, and 40s. A study from 2009 conducted by Utrecht University sociologist Gerald Mollenhorst looked at the social lives of 604 adults over the course of seven years.

It found that, during this period, only 30 per cent of those included had the same close friends as they did at the start of the study.

'Friendships breakups often happen during major life transition,' explains Baker. 'A friend may struggle with the change in dynamics in their friendships. Having shared being single or being child-free can prove to big a rift when their friend moves in with a new partner, gets married or has their first child.'

This was the case for Lauren, 31, from Glasgow, who drifted apart from a close friend after she got a new partner who

Lauren didn't get on with. 'What used to be a daily call to each other became weekly,' she says. 'As the years went by, the whole dynamic shifted and the final straw came when I called to tell her I was getting married and wanted to her to be my maid of honour. She didn't think her partner would want to come, so declined. I never thought either of us would put a partner before our friendship.'

Other circumstances that could lead to a friendship breakup include major life events or traumas – and one person feeling unsupported or let down by a friend when they needed them the most.

This was the case for Josie, 24, from Surrey. 'In the wake of the murder of George Floyd in 2020, I was really struggling,' she says. 'For context, I'm bi-racial, and this period of time was a real point of reckoning for a large number of my friendships. My best friend at the time I had only seen once that year because I had to come home from the States and then we pretty much went into lockdown a week after that.

'A few days after the killing of George Floyd, I received a text from her telling me about her university results. Of course I was really happy for her, but the overwhelming feeling I had was one of finality. How could she have said nothing to her friend of 18 years about what was going on in the world at that moment in time? How could she not have imagined the pain and hurt that I was going through?'

Occasionally, breaking up with a friend can be beneficial, particularly if this was someone who wasn't bringing positivity into your life.

'Friendship breakups can be beneficial when someone commits to changes in how they live their life,' adds Baker. 'For example, the friendships based around clubbing or drunken nights out become less appealing when someone's priorities change. Old friends might well be aggrieved at the loss of a friend they have pigeonholed as their good-time partner in crime.'

That said, the feeling of loss that comes as the result of a friendship breakup can still be deeply painful, regardless of whether or not you were the one who chose to end the relationship.

It's a feeling akin to grief, says Lucy Herd, grief recovery specialist. 'Contrary to what you may have heard, grief can be the result of many different kinds of loss,' she explains. 'This includes a friendship breakup, which can be every bit as emotional and real as the pain caused by a bereavement or another loss.'

The trouble is that friendship breakups aren't really something that are spoken about with the same gravitas as romantic breakups, which can exacerbate painful feelings, and possibly even add a degree of shame to them.

'Society places a lot of emphasis on relationship breakups between couples but when a friendship ends it can be just as painful or perhaps more depending on the circumstances,' says Dee Holmes, counsellor at the charity Relate.

'Our peers have a huge impact on our lives and who we become as people. We confide in them about issues we wouldn't tell our parents and the belief is often that while romantic relationships come and go, friendship is for life. This means when it doesn't work out in this way it can be really painful.'

When it comes to recovering from a friendship breakup, Holmes suggests initially examining why it happened.

'If you're not sure and you're keen to repair the friendship, you could ask your friend if they are willing to meet or chat things through,' she suggests.

> '**Contrary to what you may have heard, grief can be the result of many different kinds of loss, including friendship breakups**'
> – Lucy Herd, grief specialist

'They may say no and if so, it's important to respect their decision, but you could say if they change their mind they are welcome to contact you in the future.'

If the relationship is beyond repair, Holmes suggests either seeking support via counselling or trying to find other ways to move forward and accept that this person is no longer in your life.

'Some people just enter our life for a season, as they say, whereas other friendships will be for life. It's important to invest in our relationships and friendship is no different but if things feel one-sided or toxic it may be worth asking if the friendship is right for you. If you can't resolve it maybe it's time to move on.'

10 December 2021

Write...

Write a letter to a friend who you have drifted away from or fallen out with to explain why you think the friendship ended (this can be a real, or imaginary situation). Find issues on both sides of the friendship that you could have worked harder on, don't just find faults in your friend's behaviour, explore how you may have made errors too.

The above information is reprinted with kind permission from *The Independent*.
© independent.co.uk 2023

www.independent.co.uk

Dating

Chapter 2

What's the psychology behind first love?

By Nikka Celeste

All of us have our first love. We either fall in love too young or too old but we all have our first love. That special someone who makes us experience love in an intense and special way for the very first time. Also, is it the kind of love that made us experience a different kind of hurt and pain for the first time? But have you ever wondered why first love is always special and difficult to forget? As the famous quote says: 'First love never dies.'

First love is the first dose of addiction

According to the study carried out by Helen Fisher in 2005 on the fMRI of couples in love, romantic love is primarily a motivation system, rather than an emotion, that can be similar to what we experience during addiction.

There are several hormones and neurotransmitters that are involved or are released when we are in love. These are oxytocin, dopamine, and norepinephrine.

Oxytocin, which is also called the 'love hormone', is responsible for feelings of attachment and intimacy. It helps bond people closer together, it's what keeps some people monogamous, it can lower your inhibitions, and it can help you become more open and trusting of others. It is also the same chemical that bonds mothers and children.

Dopamine, on the other hand, is a neurotransmitter that is strongly associated with emotions, pleasure, and reward and in modulating the immune system. This is where the 'addiction' part of love comes in. When this hormone is released, it activates the reward centre of the brain which causes a 'motivation-reward' effect. Thus, we seek out the reward of love even through obstacles that may be dangerous or painful (a cheating partner, an abusive partner, etc.)

Norepinephrine is a drug that is used by medical experts to treat low blood pressure (hypotension) and heart diseases. It is similar to adrenaline and dopamine, which produces a racing heart and excitement. It is released in the first stages of love either lust or infatuation. According to Helen Fisher, these two chemicals – dopamine and norepinephrine – produce elation, intense energy, sleeplessness, craving, and focused attention.

Researchers at UCL discovered that people in love have lower levels of serotonin (a hormone that acts as a neurotransmitter which helps relay signals from one area of the brain to another). Low levels of serotonin are found in people diagnosed with OCD (obsessive-compulsive disorders) which may be the reason why those in love 'obsess' about their partners.

First love leaves an 'imprint' on the sensory areas of the brain

Since there are multiple studies that confirmed that our brains experience 'addiction' when we're in love, falling in love for the very first time is important because it is the foundation and, most of the time, we experience this kind of love during adolescence when our brain is still developing.

Cognitive scientists at MIT explain that we experience peak processing and memory power at around age 18 and this is the time when we experience a lot of firsts, including our first love.

Another psychologist also says that most people experience a 'memory bump' between the ages of 15 and 26. This memory bump happens at a time when we are experiencing all kinds of firsts, such as the first kiss, having sex, driving a car, etc. and later in life, these memories tend to be more impactful because they occurred when our memory was at its peak.

According to Rose Bear, these memories leave hormonal imprints that cause the life-long effects we all experience. The hormonal interactions are imprinted in the sensory areas of the brain at a time when the neurological developments we are experiencing are forming who we are as individuals. Thus triggering us to recall our first love whenever we see them on social media, or whenever a certain song plays in our playlist that makes us remember them.

Your first love affects all your relationships after

According to April Davis, a matchmaker and founder of LUMA (Luxury Matchmaking), first love often feels so intense it could lead to someone believing that they loved their first more than others. They'll long for the intense feelings they had when they were in their past relationship and look for that feeling in everyone they meet after. When they don't find it, they might find themselves looking to rekindle things with their ex.

However, according to Davis, first love isn't going to be the best or deepest love. It is because of the intensity of the first love that could translate someone a feeling that they loved that person more in their memory.

Also, according to Davis: 'Your first love will affect all your relationships after because of what it teaches you. For instance, you'll learn for the first time that you can be wanted and desired. You'll also learn how you want to be treated by another person. When you end the relationship, you'll learn what heartbreak feels like.' And as they say, there is no heartbreak that hits you like the first time.'

According to a 2017 study, 71% of people are able to heal from a breakup within a span of three months after the relationship has ended. In this context, healing means self-rediscovery for the participants. Thus, creating the famous 'three-month rule' in a relationship.

Also, first love is often marked by a period of personal growth and development, a time of new experiences, and facing your fears. As a result, the relationship helps shape who you are and how you proceed through the world and may represent the first time you allowed someone else's influence to have such a significant impact on who you are.

Takeaway

Remember, these are just several reasons why first love is hard to forget. However, just because your first love is hard to forget, it doesn't mean that it's the only true love you will ever have. For most people, it's a learning experience. Take this experience as a lesson and as a sign pointing you on the right path in your journey of finding the right person.

Nikka Celeste is a relationship and wellness expert.

11 January 2023

The above information is reprinted with kind permission from Psychreg.
© 2014–2023 Psychreg Ltd

www.psychreg.org

What is love?

By Canse Karatas, (MBACP)

Explaining love is like describing what water tastes like. Everyone's experience will be completely different. Some will deny it and some will chase it. Then there are the ones completely besotted or recovering from it. So, how do you know if what you're experiencing is really love if we cannot define it simply?

As my background is in psychology, I can confirm love is actually biologically proven. When we experience it, there is a flood of hormones released in our bodies. Chocolate really does make us happy as it releases the same hormones. Contrary to what we believe, love is not held in our hearts; it's parts of the brain that are activated by the hormones.

From a relationship point of view, there are lots of different kinds of love that we encounter. Usually, the initial love we experience is from our parents. This extends to siblings, and then wider family. As we connect with others and build friendships, we can grow close. Some people have a 'first love' or some don't experience romantic love until later in life. Marriages. Children. Pets. From a different perspective places, food or music.

Now from a psychotherapy point of view, when a client is in turmoil there can be many reasons for this. A main cause can refer back to those first relationships with our parents. These attachments affect our development and should we not receive love, attention or mirror what we learn we can spend our whole lives stuck in a cycle of unhealthy relationships. Searching and projecting these insecurities. For people who have experienced abuse of any kind in childhood, this can affect emotional regulation but also result in avoidant attachments too.

I am by no means an expert on love. However, I see clients every day that give me an idea of all the things that go right or wrong in relationships. Themes for things that go wrong are:

- a lack of honest communication and appreciation
- outgrowing friends or partners but not owning that and allowing it to become toxic
- bad timing in someone's life
- patterns of behaviour being played out from childhood or previous hurts

Often, people will persevere and try to force it but, eventually, that does even more damage.

The things I see in healthy romantic relationships is when there appears to be a deep emotional connection. Along with that, all the core values and life goals align. No two people will ever completely agree on everything but the big stuff has got to be from the same priorities. Characteristics like honesty, commitment, laughter and passion.

My advice on love of any kind is to evaluate your relationships. Obviously, there are a million things to explore - I have just covered a handful. Question everything. How can you enhance the positive ones even more? Maybe there are ones you just need to let go of to make room for really special ones to make their way into your life. Most importantly, knowing yourself and taking everything into account doing what makes you truly happy.

14 July 2022

The above information is reprinted with kind permission from Counselling Directory
© 2023 Happiful

www.counselling-directory.org.uk

How do you know when you're in love, not just infatuated? Five signs to spot

By Sian Bradley

Falling in love is one of the most exciting and terrifying things humans can experience.

Romantic love is the subject of songs, movies, TV shows for a reason, but how do you know when you feel 'it'?

That head-over-heels feeling can be hard to explain, and everyone will experience love differently – but if you are questioning whether this is love that you're feeling or a fleeting infatuation, there are some tell-tale signs to look out for.

But before we get into the signs that you may be in love, let's define what that four -letter word is.

It's such a powerful feeling that the rational brain can take a back seat sometimes (ever heard someone say their 'head's gone' when talking about falling for someone?) yet trying to explain this in concrete terms is difficult.

Why? Love isn't a feeling, not really.

What is love?

Scientifically speaking, love is a chemical reaction. Helen Fisher, an anthropologist at Rutgers University, has been researching the biological bases of love for decades.

Looking at MRI scans of smitten folks, she found that when we are falling in love, our brain is flooded with dopamine and oxytocin. 'Romantic love is primarily a motivation system, rather than an emotion,' she concludes. This has a few impacts.

First, you begin to idolise your beloved, thinking there is no one else like them. You may get blinkers, and not feel anything for anyone else, as practising monogamy can drive up dopamine – the neurotransmitter responsible for attention and focus.

Find yourself realising that everything you see reminds you of them? You can blame dopamine and norepinephrine, a chemical associated with memory, for being unable to think about anything else when you're falling for someone.

This is according to a 2013 study in the journal *Motivation and Emotion*, which found that being in love prevents people from focusing on other information.

Love may be biological, but that doesn't make it any less real. What it does mean is that we may be getting carried away because of addictive chemicals.

That mushy oxytocin feeling can come on quickly, as an evolutionary drive tells us to mate with a compatible partner (hot!), but is that love, or lust?

Love is a unique experience

'There's no lightbulb moment when it comes to love,' says Dr Laura Vowels, principal researcher and sex therapist at sex therapy app Blueheart. Instead, it grows over time, based on a foundation of mutual respect, ongoing communication, and healthy levels of trust.

Being 'in love' is a slippery concept, as it is a unique experience and can mean different things to different people, Dr Vowels argues.

In series eight of Love Island, Tasha asks fellow contestant Ekin-Su how she can know if she is in love. Ekin Su replies that you 'know' when you 'stop thinking about yourself and start thinking about them more than you. You become obsessed with things you weren't obsessed with before, like their BO, their scent, the little things they do'.

Sorry Ekin-Su, but these aren't signs of love, says trauma and relationship therapist Lizandra Leigertwood – but she understands why it might feel like it is.

There are phases to falling in love and this describes the first one, she adds. 'This is known as limerance or being in infatuation or the lust phase of a relationship,' Lizandra tells Metro.co.uk.

'It's during this time that time where we experience higher love chemicals like oxytocin and dopamine. These feelings are highly addictive and can be where we can become obsessed.'

In these early days, it's easy to ignore red flags and see things through 'rose-tinted glasses instead of the reality of what is actually happening,' Lizandra adds.

It can explain why your mate seems to be obsessed with someone who is an objectively terrible person.

This feeling can be addictive (our brains are full of chemicals that make us feel good, after all), so some will keep seeking out this early stage without ever seeing it through into a lasting relationship, Lizandra explains.

The signs that we are in love rather than lust are much less sexy…

It's lasted beyond the honeymoon period

No one can put a time limit on love, and some people say they knew they loved their lifelong partner within a few weeks or months. However, to know for real whether this is love or infatuation, time is your friend.

'We know that we are not just infatuated with our love interest when it goes beyond those first few months,' Lizandra says. 'This is why it's always a good idea to get to know someone really well to work towards building intimacy and trust.'

It needs to be deeper than thinking about them all the time, Lizandra adds, which can be unhealthy.

It's easy to get sucked into the big romantic declarations when you're feeling all the excitement of seeing some new, but you know you are in love when it's more than that.

You can tell them how you feel

'The main hallmarks of a truly loving relationship are trust, communication and respect,' explains Dr Laura Vowels. If you can't be honest with someone and trust that they will care about your feelings, it's probably not love.

She continues: 'Remember those early relationship anxieties about whether you're coming on too strong, or whether you're funny enough?

'In a genuinely trusting, loving relationship, those feelings should dissipate and both partners should be comfortable in and sure of each other's affections.'

Communication is 'the bedrock of successful partnerships', Dr Laura says, arguing that 'it's hard for love to truly flourish if a couple hasn't figured out how to properly and meaningfully communicate.'

If you can do everything with your partner but talk to them about how you feel, it may be time to call it a day and find someone who makes you feel safe enough to open up.

Another important question to ask is whether you feel respected, and respect your partner. Sure, they say all the right things, gush about your two being soulmates and makes you feel all warm inside, but do they value you as a human being?

'A lack of respect for one another's opinions, bodies, and emotions will erode romantic relationships, so make sure you're seeking this out in a partner,' Dr Vowell advises.

It's easy-going

Don't listen to pop culture that tells you nothing good comes easy – love should feel easy. That doesn't mean you never have disagreements or have doubts but it shouldn't feel like a slog.

When you love someone, it comes naturally, and you won't find yourself excusing their bad behaviour and the fact that you feel terrible 'because you love them'.

'A feeling of calm or safety during the relationship is a healthy sign,' Lizandra says.

'It's also very instinctual, as long as you're attuned to the right signs of healthy love and not getting caught up in the whirlwind of excitement that will eventually fade,' she adds.

You want to do things for them

Think about how we treat our best friends. We do things for them to make them feel loved and appreciated, whether that is buying them something when they are sad, organising their birthday celebration or just texting them to ask how they are.

Romantic relationships are no different.

You may know you are in love when you start doing little things for them: cooking them breakfast while they sleep in, buying them something because it reminded you of them, organising a cute date night to spend quality time with them.

If you want to be real with yourself, you shouldn't be doing this to 'score points' or try to convince someone you are worth being with. That's not healthy!

Instead, you find yourself thinking of their needs and wellbeing, Lizandra adds.

So, you do the washing up for them not because you want to hold it against them in a later argument or prove yourself to be some perfect partner, but because you know they are rushing off to work and will appreciate coming home to a clean kitchen.

You want the best for them

Pop culture likes to feed us this narrative that being in love means you will fight to stay with them no matter what, even if it means they have to turn down a dream job, cut off friends, move countries or change themselves in some way.

However, true love isn't possessive. A sign of being in love is truly wanting the best for them, Lizandra explains.

So, you'll encourage them to pursue their dreams and go for what will make them happy, even if it means you won't work out. Now that is truly romantic.

2 July 2022

The above information is reprinted with kind permission from *Metro*.
© 2023 Associated Newspapers Ltd

www.metro.co.uk

Healthy relationships

What makes a relationship safe and healthy?

There's no set time to be in a relationship, but if you do feel ready to start one, it's important to think about how you feel. Relationships can bring out the best in us, make us feel happy and naturally make us want to spend more time with the other person.

But sometimes it can be confusing and difficult to assess whether you're in a healthy relationship, or to know when things aren't quite right

Feeling safe, emotionally and physically, is an essential foundation for any intimate relationship. A safe relationship should be supportive and accepting, and you should be able to share your feelings without fear. Sometimes, a relationship may start safe, but become increasingly unsafe, making it harder to identify when the relationship is no longer healthy. However, it is important that your relationship, be it with a romantic partner, your parents or friends, should enhance your life and elevate the happiness you already have.

If there is any point that you feel a relationship has become unsafe or unhealthy, you should reach out to someone immediately to get support.

What makes a relationship healthy?

There is no perfect formula for making a relationship healthy, but there are some key things that you should consider:

- Mutual Respect – you may not agree on everything and that's normal, but you should always treat each other with respect.

- Compromise – we all have different opinions or views. Compromise is about being willing to give and take in order to come to a place of understanding.

- Honesty – it's important to be open and truthful, not knowingly misinforming or misleading each other. This shouldn't, however, be a licence to be rude or hurtful.

- Trust – trusting yourself and the other person includes feeling safe physically and emotionally and having the confidence to confide in and rely on them.

- Communication – good communication is crucial: talking to each other, speaking honestly and openly, and respecting each other's wishes.

- Individuality – one person shouldn't be trying to control the other in a healthy relationship. You should be comfortable being yourself.

How can I create a healthy relationship?

Here are some ideas for both you and your partner to discuss and consciously act upon to prevent the relationship becoming unhealthy or unsafe:

- Take an interest in your partner's passions and values. Try not to judge them, even if their beliefs may not align your own, and take the time to see their perspective from beyond your own.

- Try to keep communication as open as possible. Communication is key to forming the basis of respect, trust and honesty in a relationship. It's important to maintain an open, non-offensive dialogue, true to yourself and each other.

Our top tips!

There's no need to rush

You may feel like you're the only one not in a relationship, but don't rush or force yourself into anything. People feel ready for relationships at different points in their lives – don't compare your timeline on anyone else or feel pressured by others' expectations.

Focus on your own needs

Your wellbeing is important, so make sure you are sleeping and eating well and exercising regularly. If you find that a relationship is draining you, taking care of yourself can bring clarity and perspective.

Remember the importance of consent

You should always feel comfortable saying 'yes' or 'no'. Even if you agreed to something previously, you can change your mind. It's also really important to make sure that anyone you are in a relationship with is consensual as well.

- Be supportive of your partner. Offering reassurance and encouragement helps to nurture a sense of safety in the relationship.
- Respect each other's privacy. Safe and healthy relationships require space; you don't have to share and do everything with your partner. Taking the time to meet with friends separately and be independent fosters strength in the relationship.

Spotting the signs of an unsafe relationship

You feel afraid
You may start to feel afraid to disagree with your partner or to do certain things for fear of how your partner will react. For instance, you may not openly disagree with your partner because you believe it would spark confrontation and conflict.

You feel defensive
You may become defensive in response to how others view your relationship. This can be a sign of a troubled relationship since you are permanently trying to defend yourself against potential criticism, shaming or rejection.

Imbalance of power
Your partner should be your equal, but this is not the case if you are always seeking your partner's approval out of fear or obedience. A power imbalance often occurs in relationships where one partner has financial or psychological control.

Feeling the pressure
Feeling pressured can come in many forms. If your partner makes you feel guilty when you want independence or time to do your own thing, this is not a positive sign. Your partner may also pressure you to do things that you don't want to do.

Losing interest
You've stopped doing things that make you happy and healthy. Reminiscing about the things you used to do is a warning sign. A safe and respectful partner would allow you to pursue your passions outside of the relationship without even thinking about it.

Feeling questioned
If your partner questions everything you do or makes you feel insecure, this may indicate controlling or abusive behaviour. You should not feel like you are constantly being questioned in your relationship; instead, you should feel safe to do whatever you want.

Feeling untrusted
Demanding trust, without giving you any trust is a key way for someone to maintain control. If a partner demands your trust, but has done little to earn it, or makes you feel like they are always in the right and you are always in the wrong, this can be a warning sign.

I think I might need some help... what do I do?

Being in an unsafe or unhealthy relationship will often leave people feeling helpless and isolated. You are probably thinking that nobody could understand your experience and that you can't ask anyone for help. That is wrong. People do understand and you can talk to someone to get the help that you need. Never be afraid of getting help in these situations.

Get support!

If you are in a difficult situation, reach out to somebody and get the support you need.

Speak to us

You don't need to suffer in an unsafe relationship in silence. You may feel alone, you may feel scared and you may feel like we won't understand. However, it is really important that you reach out and speak to someone. If you are struggling, our mentors will be able to talk to you and help you out.

Speak to the Police

Unhealthy relationships can often include violence or other criminal acts. If you are scared and feeling stuck because of violent or emotional abuse, reach out to the police. They will be able to keep you safe.

Speak to somebody you trust

Speaking to somebody that you trust is really important. Having someone who knows what is going on means that you have someone to go to when you are feeling unhappy or unsafe. Reach out to a friend or a parent.

What if I want to end the relationship?

If you do find you want to leave a relationship for any reason, don't feel guilty. It can be hard to do, but having a plan can help. You should feel free to end the relationship if you want to. Think about what you want to say in advance and meet somewhere with others around for your own safety.

Don't be hard on yourself – you can ask people you trust for advice and guidance, and spend time doing things you enjoy to distract yourself. If you are trying to leave an unsafe relationship, consider the following:

- They probably won't change, no matter how many times they say it.
- Never make excuses for your partner, and have the courage to walk away.
- Reach out to your support network; they can keep you grounded.
- Consider keeping a journal to help document any incidents.
- Reconnect with hobbies and activities that you enjoy to take your mind off of it.

The above information is reprinted with kind permission from Teenage Helpline.
© 2023 Teenage Helpline

www.teenagehelpline.org.uk

Relationship red flags

People talk about red flags in relationships – but just what are they? Relationship red flags are clues to toxic or unhealthy behaviour between you and your partner. This article will look at some of those behaviours and how you can spot them and deal with them.

When you first start dating someone it can be easy to ignore any toxic behaviour and only focus on the positives, but there are some things that should not be ignored in order to have a healthy and respectful relationship.

Controlling or jealous behaviour

We can all be a little jealous that our partner is paying attention to someone or something else outside of our relationship. But how do we know when it is a problem? When your partner starts to try to control who you are friends with, what you wear, or control your time, then its a definite warning sign for further emotional abuse.

Lack of communication

Whilst sending millions of messages to you all day can be a hint of controlling behaviour, another thing to look out for is when your partner ignores you or takes days to get back to you. Communication is key to a good relationship, and you will probably find that you will both need to work at a level of communication that you are both happy with.

Gaslighting

Gaslighting is a form of manipulative behaviour that a person uses to gain control over another person. This usually happens very gradually so you don't notice that it is happening. A gaslighter will make you doubt yourself and question everything. They will try to confuse you and ask you to prove that you are correct. They will also make you believe that others are lying to you and try to confuse you so eventually you will depend on them for everything.

Love-bombing

Similar to gaslighting, the love-bomber partner will eventually be in a position of control, but instead of breaking down your self-esteem they in fact do the opposite. By showering you with love, affection, compliments and gifts, the partner will gain your trust completely, and then try to break you down. This is often when the abuse, or gaslighting will begin. Of course, at first it may just be infatuation and the partner may be trying to impress you, but if you feel that it's all to much or moving too fast, you need to set boundaries.

'Crazy Exes'

Exes are usually exes for a reason – but if a new partner seems hung up on their ex or the way that the relationship broke down, this may be a warning sign. Pay attention to the language used when talking about an ex-partner; if they show no respect for them that may mean that you will become their next 'crazy ex'.

They don't like your friends or family

If your partner tries to drive a wedge between you and your family, or stop you from seeing your friend's then you should take this as a big warning sign. Whilst we don't have to get on with everyone, we can at least be civil, but if they are unable to do this and show an extreme dislike for your other loved-ones then they are probably trying to get you to just spend time with them so they have control over you.

Your friends or family don't like them

Mums are always right. As much as we don't want to believe this, our parents or carers have been there and done that. They also are the ones that usually know us best (along with our friends). So they can usually spot the red flags before we can! If your friends or family try to tell you of any concerns, don't brush them off, they have probably spotted unhealthy behaviour and want you to be aware.

Of course, sometimes people can try to sabotage a relationship, but listen to what they have to say, and then speak to someone else you trust to see if they have the same concerns. If more than one person has the same worries then it may be a good idea to listen to them and see if these concerns can be resolved.

Ultimately, you should trust your gut feelings. If there are any doubts or niggles then speak to them. If they dismiss your feelings then it may be time to move on. Sometimes though, especially if you both are in your first relationship and just learning how relationships work, you will be able to set boundaries and say what you want from the relationship.

7 relationship red flags

Controlling/jealous behaviour

Lack of communication

Love-bombing

Gaslighting

Crazy Exes

They don't like your friends or family

Your friends/family dont like them

The healthy dating advice I wish I'd had as a young person…and still need in my 30s

What wisdom can a youth leader give to young people wrestling with love, sex, and relationship drama? Author Lauren Windle weighs in with her top tips.

I can picture myself with my first boyfriend. He was 13 and I was 14 (absolute cougar). He came complete with dimples and a skateboard and every time I get a waft of Lynx Africa I think about him. I wasn't in love, in fact that relationship only lasted three weeks, but for a few short days I was relieved that my search for love could finally stop. I had found the one.

Little did I know that I would find many 'the ones' of the years, the majority would be 'the wrong ones' but I threw myself into each romantic encounter with as much enthusiasm as the last.

Since Jamie-with-the-dimples, I've had my heart broken twice, and faced many other rejections. I've also done my fair share of turning people down and cutting things off. It's the circle of life. When I survey the carnage of my early love life, I can't help but think I could have navigated things better if I'd been given a little more information to work with. I went to Sunday school every week, I'd had the church relationship chat – make sure they're Christian and don't touch them anywhere until you're married.

Armed with this and the certainty that I was far more mature than other teenagers, I ventured out into the dating world. But, shockingly, this advice left me ill equipped for what lay ahead. Here's what I wish someone had said…

1. Your value is more than your relationship status

Sounds obvious. We all know that in theory at least, right? Wrong.

People need reminding of this regularly, every day perhaps. Just because someone sitting next to you in school/church is in a relationship, doesn't mean that that person is better looking/funnier/more desirable than you are. This isn't a hierarchy system, and you are not at the bottom of it.

Your value is insanely high because you are royalty. You are the son/daughter of a king and anyone who treats you as anything less has no place in your life.

2. Make sure they're kind

Nice guys/girls don't finish last. If you have ever told someone that they are 'too nice' to date you are wrong.

Kindness should be prized, championed, encouraged and sought after – especially in a dating context.

If you struggle to find someone who is respectful, emotionally available and gentle with you attractive, you need to work out why you don't see yourself as worthy of that kind of wonderful attention.

You will eventually realise that being 'kept on your toes' isn't sexy, it's rude. But realise it today rather than after yet another upset in your 30s.

3. You think sex doesn't matter – but it does

I'm one of those rare damage control Christian speakers. I recognise that it's often silly to tell people 'just don't have sex' and 'just don't try drugs' when they're so engrained in our culture. It's why I'm always surprised when Catholic schools invite me to speak. While i think everyone would be better off if we wore our chastity belts and 'just say no' badges 24/7, i recognise that's not practical.

As a young person i was told a lot about the evils of sex. I was told it was like smooshing a peanut butter and jam sandwich together and trying to pull apart the bread again without mixing up the fillings. I thought they were old fashioned and the fun police. Or maybe just virgins who didn't know what they were missing.

'You will enjoy dating far more if you see it as an opportunity to more deeply connect with someone and find out more about them – and that's it.'

What no one ever said to me was: 'go and have sex if you want to, i won't stop you. But you should know that the pain of so intimately connecting with someone who is then gone (either the next morning or in the weeks/months to come) is indescribable.

'You should know that you'll tell yourself you're fine but you will be slowly chipping away at a part of yourself that you don't even realise you're losing.

'You should know that you'll start to get increasingly desperate to hang on to those moments of physical closeness because you will have substituted love for sex and you won't know how to put them back in their rightful place. It will feel like being perpetually disconnected.

'You should know that this will all only hit you years down the line and the damage will take a lot of reflection, prayer and upset to unpick.'

Plus, all of that in exchange for what – let's be honest – will be an awkward, inexperienced and disappointing sexual encounter anyway. Because until you really know someone, understand, respect and commit to them, you won't be able to completely sexually satisfy them.

4. Don't take dating too seriously

Having just made quite a serious point, I'll now bring it back to the fun, light-hearted and enjoyable experience dating should be. Every coffee you go on should be seen as just that – a coffee. It's so important to live in that moment and not worry about if you can marry that person or what your friends will think of them. You will enjoy dating far more if you see it as an opportunity to more deeply connect with someone and find out more about them – and that's it.

Ultimately if you feel respected and you're being respectful, you're in a good place. Chuck in a bit of crazy golf and a few flirty text messages and you're on to a winner.

29 September 2021

The above information is reprinted with kind permission from Youthscape.
© 2023 Youthscape

www.youthscape.co.uk

Are you ready for sex?

Working out whether you're ready for sex is one of life's big decisions.

It might feel like everyone around you is having sex, because that's what they are saying, but they could be making it up. Never feel pressured into having sex with anyone until both of you are ready

If you're thinking about losing your virginity or having sex with a new partner, here are 7 things to think about:

1. It's your decision

Remember, only you can decide whether or not you're ready to have sex, and it's ok to say no.

2. No means no

It's important not to pressurise anyone else to be sexually active if they don't want to be. You must respect that. No means no.

3. Do you know about the law?

The legal age of consent is 16; any younger than that and it's against the law for you to be having sex. This is true for boy/girl sex, girl/girl sex, boy/boy sex and basically for all sex, with anyone!

But when you get to 16, that doesn't mean it's necessarily the right age for you to start having sex.

4. Non-consensual sex with a person who is drunk or under the influence of drugs is rape

If a person is unconscious, or if their judgement is impaired by alcohol or drugs, legally they are unable to give consent to sex.

Having non-consensual sex with a person who is drunk or under the influence of drugs is rape.

5. Communicate with your partner about sex

It's really important to communicate with your partner about being sexually intimate so you can find out each other's likes and dislikes.

What turns one person on might make the other feel uncomfortable. It's also important to wait until you're ready to progress to sex

6. Talk about safe sex

It's vital that you talk about safe sex before you get to having sex; you need to protect yourself from STIs and the risk of unplanned pregnancy.

7. You might not be ready to have sex if.....

You feel embarrassed or uncomfortable talking about points 4 or 5 above with your partner.

8 June 2020

The above information is reprinted with kind permission from the Health for Teens/NHS.
© Crown Copyright 2023
This information is licensed under the Open Government Licence v3.0
To view this licence, visit http://www.nationalarchives.gov.uk/doc/open-government-licence/

www.healthforteens.co.uk

Sex and the law

Knowing what the law says about sex and young people will help you to understand your rights, and the rights of other young people.

There are lots of different laws in the UK that are there to protect young people.

Below are the answers to common questions young people have about the law in relation to sex and sexual activity.

Sexual activity includes:

- Kissing
- Sharing sexual messages
- Sending nude or semi-nude images or videos
- Sexual touching
- Oral sex
- Vaginal or anal sex

Sexual abuse is when someone is pressured, forced or manipulated into any form of sexual activity by someone else.

> It is illegal for anyone to sexually abuse another person – online or offline.
>
> If you have been pressured into any sexual activity you should call 101 and report this to the police. Under 18s can report online sexual abuse to CEOP.
>
> **In an emergency, call the police on 999.**

Sexual offences under UK law

There are different types of sexual offences under UK law:

Rape: The legal definition of rape is when a person forces their penis into the mouth, anus or vagina of another person when that person doesn't want them to do so.

Sexual assault: Sexual assault is when someone forces or coerces someone to engage in unwanted sexual activity or when someone is touched sexually without their consent. The touching can be done with any part of the body or even with an object.

Child sex offences: It is illegal for anyone over the age of 18 to have sexual activity with someone under 16. It is illegal to take, view, share or request nude or semi-nude images or videos of someone who is under 18.

Sexual harassment: Sexual harassment is unwanted sexual behaviour that makes someone feel upset, scared, offended or humiliated. Sexual harassment includes:

- Making unwanted sexual comments or jokes
- Exposing your private parts to somebody in public
- Sharing nudes of another person without their consent
- Sending someone unwanted nudes or sexual messages
- Sending someone pornography without their consent
- Sharing or threatening to share sexual rumours about someone
- Taking sexual photos of someone without their consent (also known as upskirting)

Sexual harassment can happen anywhere (online or offline) and to anyone (regardless of their age or gender).

Sex and the law Q&A

What is the age of consent?

The age you can legally have sex is called 'the age of consent'. In the UK it is 16 years old. This means that according to the law, only those who are aged 16 or over are able to freely agree to any sexual activity.

Is it illegal for two people under 16 to engage in sexual activity?

Sexual activity between anyone who is under 16 is illegal.

However, the law is in place to protect young people from sexual abuse. Sex between two young people under the age of 16, is often treated as a safeguarding concern. This means that young people will not be in trouble with the police. Adults (such as teachers, social workers, parents and carers) will work together to make sure the young people are safe.

It is illegal for two people under the age of 18 to share nude or semi-nude images.

Will an adult get in trouble for having sex with someone under 16?

Sex or any sexual activity between an adult and a young person aged under 16 is against the law in the UK. It is illegal for an adult to take, view, share or request nude or semi-nude images or videos of someone who is under 18. If this is brought to the attention of the police, the person over 18 could be prosecuted. The punishment would be decided by the police (and possibly the court) based on the specific circumstances of the case.

Is it illegal to take a nude and send it to someone else?

It is illegal to take a nude photo or video of anyone under 18, even if it is of yourself. It is also illegal to share it with someone else.

However, the law is there to protect young people, not criminalise them unnecessarily. If you have shared an image as a part of a consensual relationship, and this comes to police attention, the police will consider that when dealing with a case.

If you have been pressured to share an image of yourself, you will not be in trouble. The law is there to support and protect you.

Is it illegal for an adult to send a young person sexual messages?

It is illegal for an adult to send sexual messages to someone under 16 – the law calls this 'sexual communication with a child'. This can include written messages and sexual or nude photos.

Is it illegal to watch pornography if you're under 18?

It isn't against the law for a young person to look at most types of pornography. If you have watched pornography, don't feel worried or ashamed. You won't get into trouble.

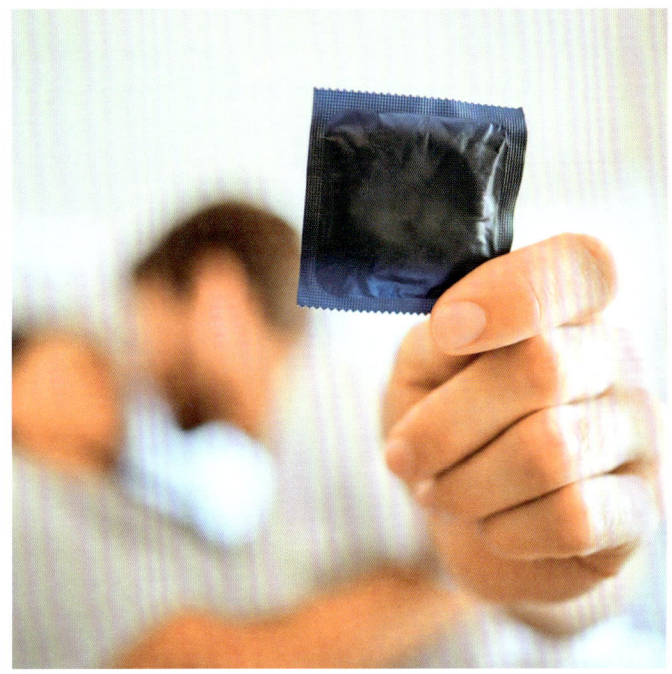

Some types of porn are illegal. It is illegal to watch porn that includes:

- Sexual abuse
- Scenes of life-threatening violence or acts that are likely to cause serious injury to a person's anus, breasts or genitals
- Sexual acts with animals or dead people

It is illegal for anyone over 18 to force or pressure a young person into watching porn.

Sexual images and videos (nudes) of under 18s are NOT pornography – these are called indecent images of children. It is illegal to create, view, store or share indecent images of children.

What happens when the police are involved?

Do teachers or the police view nudes of young people that are reported to them?

School or college staff should not intentionally view nudes or semi nudes. The person responsible for safeguarding might need to view an image, but only if it is necessary to take steps to protect the child.

The police will only view nudes of young people when they need to see the photos to protect the child and take legal action against any adults involved.

Will a young person be blamed if they make a report about sexual abuse to the police?

If someone has pressured, forced or manipulated you into any sexual activity, it is not your fault.

Any sexual activity (even if not forced or pressured) between a young person and an adult is only the fault of the adult involved.

You are the victim of a crime. The police should listen to your story without judgement.

If you're treated unfairly or inappropriately after making a police report, you can make a complaint. Support services will be able to help you with this process and make sure you get the support you need.

The above information is reprinted with kind permission from CEOP Education from the National Crime Agency.

© Crown Copyright 2023

This information is licensed under the Open Government Licence v3.0
To view this licence, visit http://www.nationalarchives.gov.uk/doc/open-government-licence/

www.thinkyouknow.co.uk

Sexting

What is sexting?

Sexting is when you send a sexual message to someone else. This could include sending nude images of yourselves, talking about sexual activities or doing sexual activities on a live stream. It can happen between partners, friends or even strangers online. Sexting can be harmless as long as you're both over 18 years old, but it can go wrong. Not everyone in a relationship takes part in sexting, so if it makes you uncomfortable, don't feel like you have to do it.

There is support available if things do go wrong, and it's important not to feel embarrassed or guilty for having to seek help. Having a nude image of yourself shared or being threatened is not your fault! Sexting should always be consensual for everyone involved. Being pressured into sending a message with sexual content is never okay. Someone may pressure you by:

- Asking you over and over again
- Bribing you with money or gifts
- Making it seem like you owe them something
- Telling you that they will be sad or hurt if you don't send them a nude, sometimes even threatening suicide or self-harm.

We are ready to start sexting... what do we need to think about?

With social media being so popular now, sexting has become a natural part of many relationships. If you and your partner or friend feel ready to start sexting, there are a few things that you should consider:

- **Sexting can be messages or images** – Whether it is sexual messages or pictures, make sure that you set your boundaries so that neither one of you goes too far.
- **Age** – Are you both over 18? If one of you (or both of you) is under 18, then you will be breaking the law by sexting. This is especially true if you share images of each other.
- **Privacy** – It is really important that you respect each other's privacy. This is an intimate part of a relationship and you should treat each other with respect.
- **Consent** – Both individuals should consent to taking part in this. Just because you have consented to something once, this does not mean that your partner can assume that you will consent every time. If either one of the people in the relationship says that they want to stop sexting, you need to stop.

I sent someone a nude and now I regret it... what do I do?

If you're worried about what might happen, there are things you can do:

- **Ask them to delete the message** – Remember that images can be saved from any app, including Snapchat.
- **Don't give in to pressure to send more** – Ignore any requests or threats that you receive to send more images. This prevents the other person from feeling that they can control your decisions and actions.
- **Reach out** – Telling someone you trust – such as a parent, friend or teacher – can be scary. However, it is an important step in seeking support and putting an end to any inappropriate conduct.
- **Report it** – If you're under 18, you can make a report to CEOP. Asking or threatening someone under 18 for nudes is illegal. If you're over 18, posting an image online without your consent is also illegal.

Somebody keeps asking me for nude pictures... what should I do?

Ask them to stop

The first thing you should do is tell them that you don't want to engage in sexting. Tell them if it makes you uncomfortable. Open, honest communication should be enough for someone to stop asking if they respect you.

> **Our top tips!**
>
> **Reach out**
> Speaking to a friend, family member, parent or teacher can be an important step in helping you cope with how you're feeling. Tell them if you regret sending a nude or have been pressured into sexting. You can also speak to one of our friendly mentors.
>
> **Don't feel ashamed**
> You'd be surprised to know how many people engage in sexting, and how many of these individuals end up seeking help. Being pressured or threatened into sexting is not your fault and there is nothing to be embarrassed about.
>
> **Block them if they're making you feel uncomfortable**
> Blocking a phone number, social media contact and even an email address is very easy. Doing this will mean the person making you uncomfortable won't be able to contact you anymore.

Use the block function

If asking them to stop sending nudes doesn't work, you can always block them. Most – if not all – social media platforms contain a block function. Similarly, you can block phone numbers and email addresses from contacting you.

Ignore them

The person asking you for these pictures may not be somebody who you want to block; or, no matter how many times you try to block them, they come back with another account. If people are persistent, don't give in; try to ignore and avoid them.

Contact CEOP

If they're still attempting to contact you, reaching out to CEOP is a good next step. CEOP is a police division that support online cases like this and will be able to help. Although this isn't confidential, they can help you.

I think I might need some help... what do I do?

Sexting can be a big part of a relationship, and is often the first sign that relationships are developing into a sexual nature. Sexual relationships are a completely natural part of life as you develop.

There are a few things that you need to consider with sexting, and sometimes it can go too far or start to make you feel uncomfortable. If something happens that you are not happy about, reach out and get support.

Get support!

If you are feeling uncomfortable with any sexual experience online, it is really important to reach out and get support.

Speak to us

Sexual relationships can be difficult to navigate at the best of times, and when you introduce sexting, they can become even more complicated. It is OK to feel uncomfortable, and you can reach out to our friendly mentors if you need to talk. There is no need to feel scared or embarrassed.

Speak to an adult

If you find yourself feeling uncomfortable or in a sticky situation, you can always talk to your parents or another trusted adult. Although you might feel nervous about telling them, they will want to support you.

Contact CEOP

If it goes too far and you feel uncomfortable (such as if somebody asks you to send them pictures when you are under 18) then this should be reported. It is likely that they are doing this to other people too. Don't feel embarrassed or ashamed in seeking help. CEOP deal with situations like this all the time.

Can I ask someone for a nude?

If you're flirting or in a relationship with someone, it can be tempting to begin sexting or ask for nudes. It's important to remember that asking for this can make someone feel uncomfortable. Before you ask, think about:

How old you both are

Remember that it's illegal to ask someone under 18 to send a nude. If you're under 18, it's illegal for you to send a nude to someone else.

Whether you've put pressure on the other person

Making someone feel guilty for not sending a nude is pressure. Remember that sexting should always be consensual and you should respect the other person's decision. If you pressure them, you cannot get consent.

If you do decide to ask them to start sexting, make sure they understand that you're not pressuring them into anything, and they have every right to say no. Explain to them that if they don't want to, you won't be upset and it won't affect your relationship. Whatever they say, you should respect their decision. Remember that if they consent to sexting – or anything else – on one occasion, this does not mean that you can assume their consent in the future.

24 December 2021

Design

Design a signposting poster to help young people find help if they are uncomfortable with requests to sext, or if they have and regret it. Include information on CEOP and how to report any images of themselves or friends.

The above information is reprinted with kind permission from Teenage Helpline.
© 2023 Teenage Helpline

www.teenagehelpline.org.uk

What is consent?

Consent is a part of our everyday lives. It is a crucial aspect of all our relationships, whether romantic, professional, or platonic. In this #YesSheCan blog, we will explore the definition of consent, its importance, and what it can look like in different settings.

What is consent?

Consent is defined as permission for something to happen or agreement to do something. Moreover, consent is an ongoing process of discussing your boundaries and what you are comfortable with. Consent can be verbal or non-verbal, such as a simple shake of the head. Consent is sober, enthusiastic, and most importantly, mutual. Even after you have consented, it is still okay to revoke your consent. Researchers found that one in every eight women do not believe they have the right to withdraw consent once the activity has started. Consent is entirely voluntary, and it is your choice whether or not to consent.

What is not consent?

Unfortunately, due to lack of education, what does and does not qualify as consent can be a bit confusing. One of the most famous phrases surrounding consent is 'No means no'. While this is true, there are many more signs as to whether or not a person is giving consent. The absence of no does not mean yes. Here are a few examples of what consent does not look like:

- Silence
- Being incapable of saying yes or no (under the influence of drugs or alcohol)
- Consent to do an activity at a different time
- Consent to something else
- Coerced consent (feeling pressure to consent)
- Clothing
- Behaviour

Consent in everyday life

Consent is a part of our everyday lives, whether we realize it or not. In our careers, romantic relationships, and friendships, we can make our boundaries clear through consent.

Consent in the workplace

In the workplace, consent can take place between colleagues as well between a subordinate and leader. Sexual harassment in the workplace is a very unfortunate reality of the world we live in today. Professional settings can cultivate consent culture by providing employees by implementing a 'zero-tolerance' policy, providing information on consent, and offering helpful resources to victims.

Consent in friendships

In our friendships, consent and boundaries can build safety and trust. Understanding our friends' boundaries is essential to a healthy friendship. By asking your friends if its okay to hug them, borrow a jumper, or share information with another friend, you can spark conversations that can have a positive, lasting impact. You can make your boundaries clear during conversations like these, as well.

Consent in relationships

In our relationships, consent cultivates healthy habits that allow for all parties to have a clear understanding of what the other person wants. Having conversations surrounding consent, outside of physically intimate settings, can enhance the respect and trust within the relationship. No matter how long the relationship has been, it is crucial to continue to ask for consent as boundaries can change.

The above information is reprinted with kind permission from Yes She Can.
© 2023 Yes She Can Ltd

www.yes-shecan.com

Sex and consent

Consent means agreeing to do something. When it comes to sex, this means agreeing to have sex or engage in sexual activity. Find out about why consent is important during sexual activity.

What is consent?

To consent means to agree to something, and the word can be used in lots of different situations. When it comes to sex specifically, to consent means to agree to have sex or engage in sexual activity.

> **What is sexual activity?**
>
> Sex or sexual activity can include kissing, sexual touching, oral, anal and vaginal sex with a penis or with any other type of object.

It's important that everyone involved in sexual activity is consenting at all times – no one should ever feel they have to do something they are not comfortable with or don't want to do. Just because you have consented to one thing doesn't mean you have consented to something else, and it's completely ok to say no or stop at any point if you don't want to continue.

Consent and the law

The Sexual Offences Act 2003 (England and Wales) defines consent as when a person 'agrees by choice and has the capacity to make that choice'.

In the eyes of the law, consent is the agreement between participants to engage in sexual activity. All those involved must have the freedom and full capacity to make that decision. Engaging in a sexual act without the person's consent is sexual violence, and is a criminal offence.

The law around consent makes consensual sex and sexual assault seem very black and white when, in reality, consent can be ambiguous and confusing.

What is sexual violence?

Sexual violence is the general term used to describe any kind of unwanted sexual act or activity. This can include:

- Rape (penetration of the vagina, anus or mouth with a penis without consent)
- Sexual assault / abuse (any act of unwanted sexual contact including rape, online grooming, domestic abuse and sexual exploitation)
- Sexual harassment (any unwanted behaviour of a sexual nature e.g sexual comments or jokes that makes you feel uncomfortable, distressed, or humiliated)
- Female genital mutilation (fgm)

What does the law mean by freedom and full capacity?

When the law uses the words 'freedom' and 'capacity' in relation to consent, it is talking about someone being able to agree to sexual activity with full understanding of what they are agreeing to, and no pressure to say 'yes'.

Another way of thinking about it is consent is someone saying 'yes' only when they really mean 'yes' because it is something they genuinely want to do. This is sometimes called 'enthusiastic consent'.

There are situations where someone might not be able to give consent because they don't have the freedom or capacity to do so. Some examples of this are:

- If the person is too drunk or high to understand what is happening. Being under the influence of drugs or alcohol may mean that someone doesn't have the mental capacity to consent to sexual activity. They may not be able to understand what they are agreeing to, even if they can say 'yes'.

- If the person is asleep or unconscious. Someone who is asleep or unconscious is not aware of what is going on and, therefore, does not have the mental capacity to consent to sexual activity.

- If a person is pressured or coerced into sexual activity. If someone is being manipulated or threatened in to sexual activity, they do not have the freedom to consent. This is because their decision is being influenced by pressure and/or fear. You can read more about dealing with pressure on the childline website. Threats could include physical violence, but also things like threatening to break-up or to share secrets or images with other people.

- If a person isn't able to withdraw consent. If someone is unable to withdraw their consent, for example if they aren't able to speak or communicate clearly, then they don't have the freedom to express consent. In short: if they can't say no, then they can't say yes either.

- If someone is under the age of consent. In the uk, the legal age of consent is 16. This means that, legally, a person under 16 is not able to consent to sexual activity because they are seen as not having the capacity to do so. It is important to remember that the law is designed to protect young people from abuse, harm or being taken advantage of by adults. It is not meant to criminalise young people and there is no intention to prosecute people under the age of 16 where both mutually agree (consent) and where they are of a similar age.

Who does consent affect?

The short answer: everyone.

Everyone needs to know about consent so they can keep themselves and other people safe. It is important for everyone to understand what it means to give and get consent, not only because anyone could experience sexual activity against their will, but because everyone also has the potential to engage in sexual activity with someone who might not want to if they don't understand how to navigate consent.

The important thing to remember is that whatever way you choose to have sex, you always need consent from all people involved. Always, every time and throughout every encounter.

You should never be pressured into or subjected to sexual activity that you don't want to do. Just as you always need to seek consent from other people, you should always have your own consent sought, and you always have the right to withhold or withdraw consent.

How to apply 'consent' to real life

The subject of consent is often approached quite simplistically as a matter of 'yes' and no'. However, this rarely matches up with people's experiences.

Similarly, understanding and defining sexual violence often relies on the extreme distinctions of 'consensual sex' or 'rape', when in reality situations can feel more complicated than this.

Even though applying consent to your own life can feel complicated, there are some ways of thinking about it that are straightforward and always true:

- It doesn't matter what your relationship with someone, how far into a sexual situation you get or how far you've gone with them before, you always have the right to change your mind and stop at any time. It's up to the other person to respect that.

- Any sort of sexual activity without consent is illegal whatever the age of the people involved and whatever their relationship.

- It's simple. You can stop sexual activity at any time, and this doesn't just have to be by saying the words 'no' or 'stop'. Consent is more than just a 'yes' or 'no' in the moment, and requires verbal and physical communication before, during and after sexual activity.

Getting help

If someone forces you to do something sexual that you do not want to do, it is never your fault and it is not ok. If this has happened to you, you should speak to someone you trust to get help and support and report what has happened.

Speaking to a trusted adult

If you need help, whatever is going on, you should try to speak to an adult that you trust. This could be someone in your family, but it could also be a teacher, midday meal supervisor, social worker or one of your friend's parents. It should be someone that you have a good relationship with and someone who you think has your best interests in mind.

Help from sexual health services

Brook services are able to offer you advice and support with all aspects of sex and relationships. Our friendly staff will not judge you or report you but will listen to what's going on and see how they can help.

If you don't have a brook service in your area, you should be able to access help and support from any sexual health service.

Other sources of help and support

There are lots of places that are able to offer help and support by phone or online:

For general help and support with anything, people under 19 anywhere in the uk can contact childline online or by calling 0800 1111.

If you or someone you know has been affected by sexual abuse, assault or violence, you can get support from victim support or rape crisis.

For medical advice, you can contact NHS 111 by dialling 111 (England and parts of Wales) or NHS 24 call 08454 242424 (Scotland)

Urgent help

If you (or someone you know) are experiencing or at risk of sexual abuse, assault or violence, you can call 999 for an ambulance, the police or any other emergency service any time of day or night if it is safe for you to do so.

The 999 emergency number covers all of the UK and is free to call from any phone.

Sexual violence statistics

Current research shows that sexual violence, including within intimate relationships, disproportionately affects women. However, anyone can experience sexual violence regardless of sex, gender, sexual orientation or age.

The Crime Survey for England and Wales (2017) estimated that 20% of women and 4% of men have experienced some type of sexual assault since the age of 16.

A US survey in 2010 found that:

- 46% of bisexual women have been raped, compared to 17% of straight women and 13% of lesbians
- 40% of gay men and 47% of bisexual men have experienced sexual violence, compared to 21% of straight men

A SafeLives report from 2018 stated that trans survivors are one of the most hidden groups of domestic abuse survivors, because there is not much research that has been done into how many trans people are affected by domestic and sexual violence.

Research from Stonewall suggests that 11% of the LGBT+ population have experienced domestic abuse in the last year; twice as high as the population as a whole (4.5% as recorded by the Crime Survey England and Wales). For bisexual women this increases to 13%, and for trans/non-binary people to 19%. For LGBT+ people who have experienced domestic abuse, 19% experience sexual violence from their partners.

The above information is reprinted with kind permission from Brook Young People.
© 2023 Brook Young People

www.brook.org.uk

Teenage boys uncertain about navigating consent and sexual culture, finds new study

While typical consent education in secondary schools may rationalise or provide a 'road map' for consent, teenage boys feel uncertain and anxious about navigating the perceived realities of youth sexual culture, according to new research from the University of Surrey.

By Dr Emily Setty

The research explores how boys are being taught about consent at school and how they relate to and interpret educational messages about consent.

The study involved classroom observations, individual focus groups with boys, and discussions with teachers. Participating schools included a co-educational academy in a relatively middle-class, monocultural (white British) semi-rural area; a boys' academy in a socioeconomically deprived urban area serving predominantly black and minority ethnic pupils; and an independent boys' school in an urban area serving a relatively socioeconomically privileged cohort.

Dr Emily Setty, author of the study and Senior Lecturer in Criminology said:

'Abstractly, most of the boys found these lessons helpful and as providing a straightforward set of strictures for them to follow. Yet, it seemed they were often framed as initiators of sex and it was clear that they struggled with some of the tensions and dilemmas that they face, as initiators, to secure consent from a sexual partner.

'I believe we need to reflect on the premise and objectives of consent education. My discussions with the boys often explored the nature of 'choice' and the constraints on choice that exist.

'Rather than hoping that knowledge will change behaviour in a linear and desired fashion, we may need to consider why it doesn't. We can then start to use consent education to enable young people to practise and develop the skills and emotional literacy required to uphold their own and one another's rights to free and informed choice.

'Education must deal with the realities of ambivalence, ambiguity, and uncertainty, rather than trying to smooth this over through rationalised consent education. The road to consensual and affirming sex and relationships is far from smooth and we need to go further in helping young people navigate the bends and bumps - both anticipated and encountered.'

Educating young people about consent in schools in England is required as part of the now-statutory Relationships, Sex, and Health Education (RHSE) curriculum.

School-related sexual violence, abuse, and harassment (SVAH) among young people is recognised as a global problem. In July 2020, the Everyone's Invited website was created, which encouraged young people to share testimonials about their experiences of SVAH in schools. There are now over 55,000 testimonials, with over 3,000 schools named. A rapid response report conducted by UK schools' regulator Ofsted followed this and detailed a worrying normalisation of SVAH in state and independent schools and colleges. It was identified that girls and gender non-conforming young people are disproportionately likely to be victims of SVAH, while boys are more likely to perpetrate SVAH.

Dr Emily Setty continued:

'Typically, RSHE about sexual consent in England educates about the law and "affirmative consent" – which places responsibility on initiators of sex to secure consent through clear and direct agreement. However, this presents consent as something to be obtained as a minimal requirement rather than to be 'enthusiastically' established, which often reduces the ability of boys to perceive themselves as having rights to their own sexual consent. Furthermore, it was found that this often creates a sense of responsibility, even burden, that may manifest in resistant and hostile attitudes.'

While the boys in the study believed that boys responsible for SVAH may have problems with impulse control and self-regulation, many of them articulated a personal lack of emotional literacy and self-knowledge. They perceived a lack of space to engage with and explore their feelings and found it difficult to know how they could express emotions during sexual interactions.

30 November 2022

The above information is reprinted with kind permission from University of Surrey.
© 2023 University of Surrey

www.surrey.ac.uk

How do young men navigate consent in a post Me Too world?

Young men are keen to talk about consent. So say sex educators, who are helping them move the conversation beyond 'no means no'.

By Franki Cookney

In a small classroom tucked away up a few flights of stone steps, two dozen young men are reflecting on their chat-up lines. 'Sometimes I've gone in and told a girl she was hot and maybe I shouldn't have,' admits one. 'I might think differently now.'

The desks have been pushed back against the wood-panelled walls and the lads are sitting around in their sportswear, discussing 'rugby culture'. In half an hour they'll be out in the chilly February night, training with Cambridge University's under-20s team. But right now, they're crammed into what is becoming an increasingly stuffy classroom to attend a workshop on masculinity.

The session is run by Good Lad Initiative (GLI), an organisation which delivers volunteer-led workshops in schools and universities on everything from male mental health, to LGBTQ+ identity, sex and consent.

No one in the room has actually used the word 'consent', but that's what they're talking about. And recognising that innocuous-seeming compliments can make women feel uncomfortable is the first step towards a more nuanced understanding of it.

Facilitator Jolyon Martin, 27, first attended a GLI workshop himself four years ago when he was still a student. 'People often do these things for social capital,' he says. 'The workshop shows them that actually no one in the room is impressed by that behaviour.'

He's noticed a move away from a 'minimum standards' approach to consent – which focuses simply on what's legal and what's not – and towards a more holistic view. He also believes the freshers arriving at university have a better attitude than some of the older students.

These conversations are to empower young men to want more for themselves

'I've been in workshops where an older guy has said something and the 18-year-olds have called him out on it,' Martin says.

For Matt Whale, consent wasn't something he gave much thought to as a teenager. 'In my head, saying "no" was in response to a violent act by a stranger, or a random man being creepy,' the 24-year-old admits.

At 18 he moved to London to study and began to hear stories that undermined this view. Friends told him about being sexually assaulted on dates. Others talked of the pressure they felt to appease their partners. 'The frequency of this has completely blown my mind,' he says.

Like most people his age, Whale's school sex ed consisted of basic biology and an assertion that 'no means no'. But as the Me Too movement and the recent conviction of disgraced Hollywood producer Harvey Weinstein shows, consent is more complicated than that.

Very few young people are taught what it means when someone equivocates, changes their mind or doesn't say anything at all. In 2018, Childline reported a 29 per cent increase in teenagers seeking advice on peer-on-peer sexual abuse. The organisation noted that callers lacked understanding about consent and how it applied within relationships. Meanwhile, a 2019 survey of 5,649 university students by sexual health charity Brook found that 56 per cent had encountered unwelcome sexual behaviour.

But while many may appear fearful or defensive about their ignorance, few are apathetic. Contrary to the typecasting, boys and young men are keen to participate in conversations about consent.

For her recent book, Boys and Sex, journalist and author Peggy Orenstein spent two years interviewing young men in the US. She feels optimistic about their willingness to discuss consent. 'I saw so much in them that was so interesting and valuable,' she said in an interview with Time magazine. 'They were really ready and eager to engage in all of these issues.'

And me

Nathaniel Cole is a London-based writer, speaker and sex educator, who works with organisations such as Sexplain UK and GLI delivering workshops to children aged 8 to 18. He says the key to opening up consent conversations with young men is not by lecturing students, but by listening. 'These conversations are not just to tell them what they've been doing wrong, but to try to empower them to want more from themselves,' he says.

This is what workshops like GLI's aim to do. 'Boys have been taught that to survive in the harsh world of dating you need to learn some tricks,' explains director of GLI, Dan Guinness. 'We want to open up space that people can say these things, then discuss what that would feel like for the other person. It's about trying to shift the perspective.'

The students attending today's workshop seem confident and engaged, but you might expect that from Cambridge undergraduates. However, youth worker Glen Wiseman, who delivers sex education in state secondary schools, says teens are just as eager to talk.

> Young men have always been fascinated about consent

'They're desperate to have these conversations,' he says. 'Whenever they're asked what they'd like to cover next, they always say they want the sexual health or relationship sessions.'

Wiseman is part of Bracknell Forest local authority's sexual health team in Berkshire. As well as facilitating discussions and offering advice, they give out free condoms, offer pregnancy tests and STI screening, and prescribe contraception.

The team runs 300 sessions a year and in 2019 saw 5,000 teenagers come through their doors. 'We've moved on from the basic consent stuff,' Wiseman says. 'We talk about accessing pleasure and communicating how you want it to be.'

Historically, relationships and sex education (RSE) in British schools has focused on the mechanics of sex and on contraception. The 1999 Teenage Pregnancy Strategy brought government funding into areas like Bracknell Forest, which had one of the highest teenage pregnancy rates in the country at the time.

Justin Hancock remembers the initiative well. He has worked with young people for more than 20 years, first as a youth and social worker and then as a dedicated sex educator. Boys' desire to talk about consent isn't new, he says; but society's realisation that those conversations matter is.

'Young men have always been fascinated about consent and wanted to talk about what it is that they're supposed to be doing,' he says. 'They've always been very aware that, generally speaking, they will have the most power in a sexual situation, and they want to make sense of it.'

As the 10-year strategy came to an end, for a lot of places the money dried up. Further cuts to local governments caused RSE to drop down the list of priorities. Continued financial support to his area allowed Wiseman and his colleagues to adapt their clinics and workshops in line with shifting attitudes and priorities, but many schools do not have that luxury.

From September 2020, RSE will become statutory in all secondary schools in England. The curriculum guidelines mention consent, but how these lessons will be taught depends on the available resources. 'Schools either don't have enough money or they're not allocating enough money towards RSE,' says Hancock. 'They're not sending their staff on training because they can't afford to pay for cover staff. And they can't afford to pay for external workshops.'

Talking the talk

Harvey Weinstein was sentenced in March to 23 years in prison, after being found guilty of a criminal sexual assault in the first degree and third-degree rape. During the trial his defence lawyer, Donna Rotunno, told the New York Times' The Daily podcast that, if she were a man, she would ask women to sign consent forms before sex.

Both the high-profile trial and Rotunno's controversial words – which outraged many – have helped to keep the topic of consent firmly in the public sphere. Generation Z boys and young men, growing up with access to a wealth of information and ideas on social media, are switched on to that.

Whale says he's never had a conversation with a group of male friends about consent, but tells me about an Instagram account he follows which has helped his understanding. Everyone interviewed for this piece agreed the Me Too movement had made a huge impression, raising awareness of consent among teenage boys, but not always in the way you might expect.

'Me Too has also had a negative effect in that boys are starting to question it and ask if it can be true,' explains Cole.

Guinness agrees: 'People get defensive. It's that idea of, "You can't do anything anymore," or, "You put your arm around someone and you go to jail".'

The key, Cole says, is to try to meet their challenges with compassion. In his 2019 talk for TedxLondon, he explained that allowing boys to talk about their fears and frustrations was a crucial part of consent education.

According to Cole, society is finally cottoning on to how valuable education around consent can be; and where schools have brought it in, they've seen good results. 'More talks and workshops are being booked proactively,' he says. 'Rather than waiting for boys to go down a certain path, they want to have the conversation now.'

24 April 2020

The above information is reprinted with kind permission from Positive News, in association with Franki Cookney.

© 2023 Positive News Publishing Ltd

www.positive.news

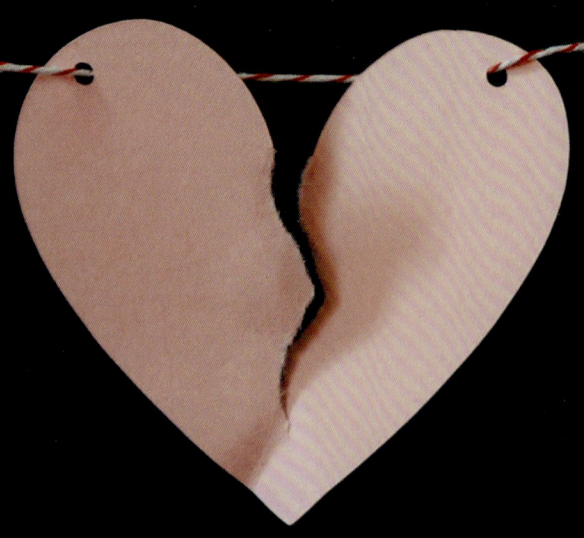

How to break up with someone... nicely

The end of a relationship is never easy, but there are some things you can do to make the process easier for both parties.

Whether you have been in the relationship for a few weeks or a few years it's still hard to be the one that says that they want to end things. There are many reasons why people break up. People grow apart, or realise that they aren't as well matched as they thought they were. Sometimes, it may just not be the right time for one of you to be in a relationship, you may want different things. Its not always arguments or upset that causes a relationship to break up, although this can be a valid reason.

Breaking up is hard, and it does hurt, but it's often for the best. Unfortunately, most people go through a break-up or two through their lives and it never gets any easier.

Here are some tips on how to break up in a kind and respectful way:

Be honest

Tell them why you want to break up, but don't lay all the blame or fault on them. Focus on your feelings and how the relationship is no longer meeting your needs. Explain your reasons for breaking up, but don't make excuses or beat around the bush, you need to be honest and clear. If you make out that its all their fault, or point out all their failings ,they will go on the defensive and it will turn into a huge argument, which you want to avoid. Of course, emotions may be high, but if you stay calm and collected, then tensions shouldn't rise.

Also, don't give them false hope of a reconciliation. You should be clear that this is the end of the relationship, and that you are not interested in having a break (remember Ross and Rachel in *Friends*?) or reconsidering the relationship.

Do it in person

Don't ghost someone – its not fair on either of you. For the recipient of the ghosting it's hurtful and the feelings of rejection, grief and guilt are overwhelming. For both of you, there's no sense of closure as the relationship is ended abruptly and without conclusion.

By being face-to-face with someone that you are breaking up with shows them that you respect them enough to talk things through, and let them have their say and express how they feel.

Don't do it over text, phone, email, or social media.

The only time it is acceptable to break up with someone remotely, is if you feel unsafe to do it in person.

Pick a good time and place

If you feel safe enough to do so, then choose a place that is in a neutral location. Make sure you are able to get home by yourself, so you don't get stranded, or have to rely on them taking you home. Somewhere like a park or coffee shop is ideal, busy enough that you are not completely alone, but private enough that people won't be listening in on your conversation. A public place may mean that tempers do not rise tpo quickly. Don't do it at their home or yours, where they, or you, might feel trapped.

If you are worried about their reaction, then maybe have a friend close by that can come to your aid if need be.

Try not to break up with someone when they're busy, stressed, or going through a hard time.

Choose a time when you're both calm and relaxed. However, sometimes its necessary to break up when things are difficult and you need to make sure that you are not stuck in a relationship as you are worried about hurting their feelings, or their reaction.

Be compassionate and empathetic

Breaking up with someone can be very upsetting for both of you. It can also be painful as heartbreak can trigger the same part of the brain as physical pain. Try to put yourself in their shoes and understand how they might feel. Don't be cold or indifferent, but don't be overly emotional or dramatic either. Be gentle and supportive, but firm and consistent. Make sure the conversation doesn't go on too long, and don't pick out all their faults as then they may believe that if they change their behaviour you will take them back.

Give them some space

After the break-up its best to cut off all contact, at least for a while, to allow you both to heal. Give them space to deal with their feelings and to adjust to being single again. Don't text, call, email, or stalk them on social media. And if they do that to you, make sure you set firm boundaries and also respect any boundaries they may set.

You may need to block them if they continue to contact you, and don't be surprised if they block you. Don't text, call, email, or stalk them on social media. Don't hang out with them as friends or hook up with them as exes. Thats a surefire way to make the situation even more difficult as they, or you, might get the wrong idea and think that the relationship will start again. Its not healthy for either of you.

You may choose after some time to remain friends, but this isn't something that will always happen. At best, you will both be amicable towards each other.

Digital detox

As well as giving your now ex space, consider having a detox of your digital life. If necessary, have a cull of friends on social media. Sort though your photos and videos, if you don't want to delete them, you can always 'hide' them so others can't see or comment on them.

Unfollow or unfriend them on social media. The temptation to have a look at their account and see what they are up to may be too much, and they may either post hurtful things about you, try to 'show you what you are missing', or try to make you jealous. If you need to, block them. That way they won't be able to contact you directly and it removes the temptation of stalking them on social media.

Learn and grow

Just because you have broken up with someone doesn't mean you have to forget them completely. You will have spent good times together and the lessons you learned, and the growth you experienced together.

Hopefully, you will both learn from your relationship, and when you begin your next one, you will know what you want from the relationship and how you can both be on the same page.

Can you stay friends with your ex?

YouGov reveals how Britons navigate the dangerous waters of break-ups.

By Isabelle Kirk

The ending of relationships can be an emotional minefield for all parties involved. Should you stay friends with your ex? Do you have to give back any presents they gave you? Can your family and friends stay friends with your ex, even if you're broken up? A new YouGov poll shows how Britons feel about 'ex etiquette'.

Just 8% of Britons with ex-partners are friends with all their exes

Among all Britons with an ex-partner, just 8% are friends with all of their exes, and half (51%) are not friends with any of their previous partners. Around a third (37%) say they are friends with one or some, but not others.

Men are more likely than women to say they are friends with at least one of their ex partners, by 51% to 40%. More than half of women (56%) say they are not friends with any of their exes, compared to 45% of men.

Britons are split on whether they would prefer to remain friends with an ex-partner

When relationships end with no significant wrongdoing by either party, Britons with an ex tend to prefer to remain friends – as long as they were the ones to end the relationship.

A little less than half (44%) of Britons with an ex would prefer to remain friends if they themselves had ended the

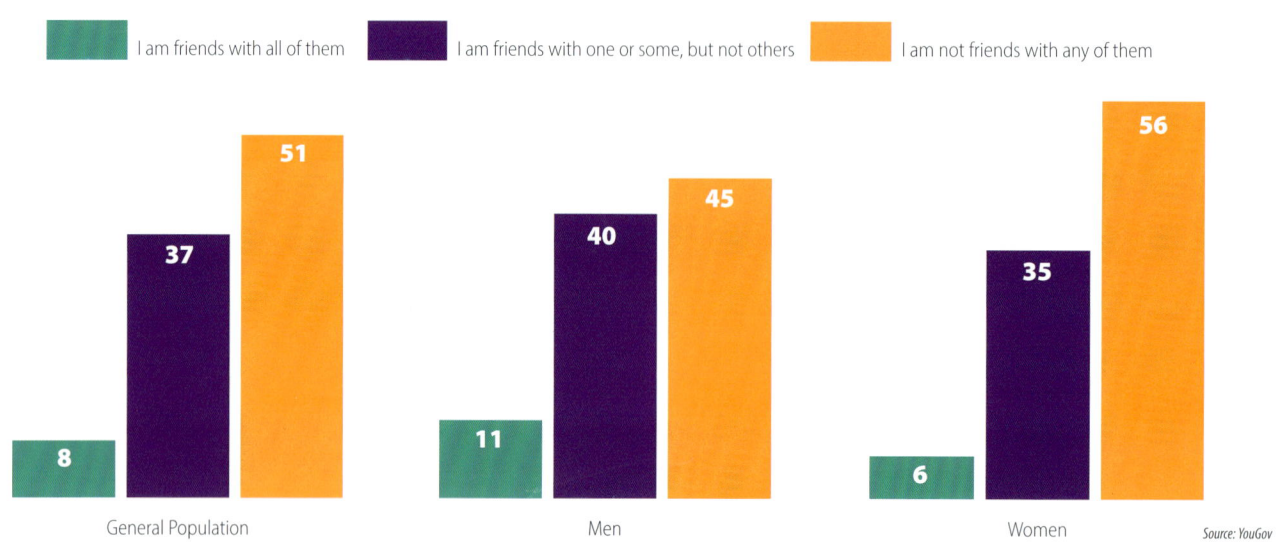

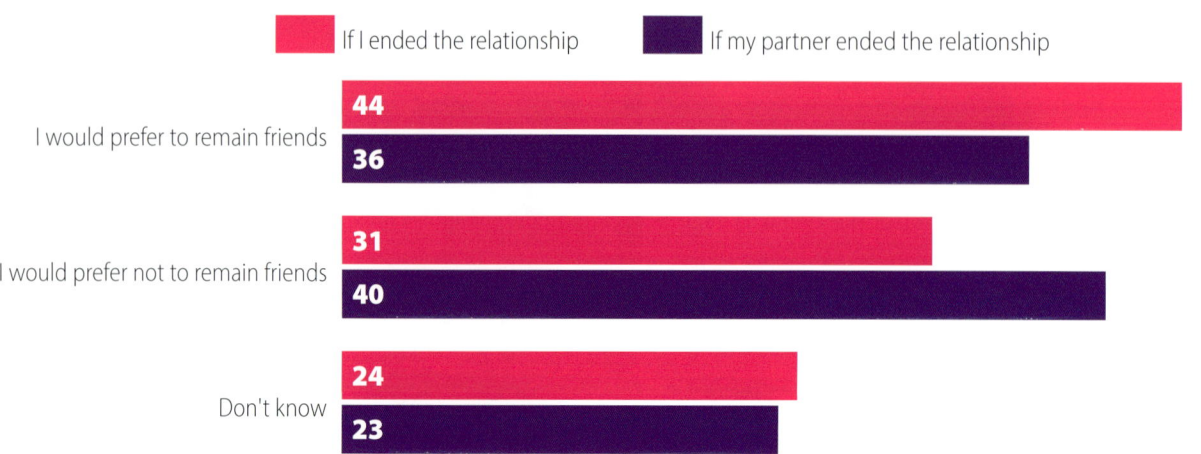

Would you be comfortable with a partner of yours being friends with an ex of theirs? Not if they're best friends, say Britons

Generally speaking, do you think you would be comfortable or uncomfortable with a partner of yours being...? %

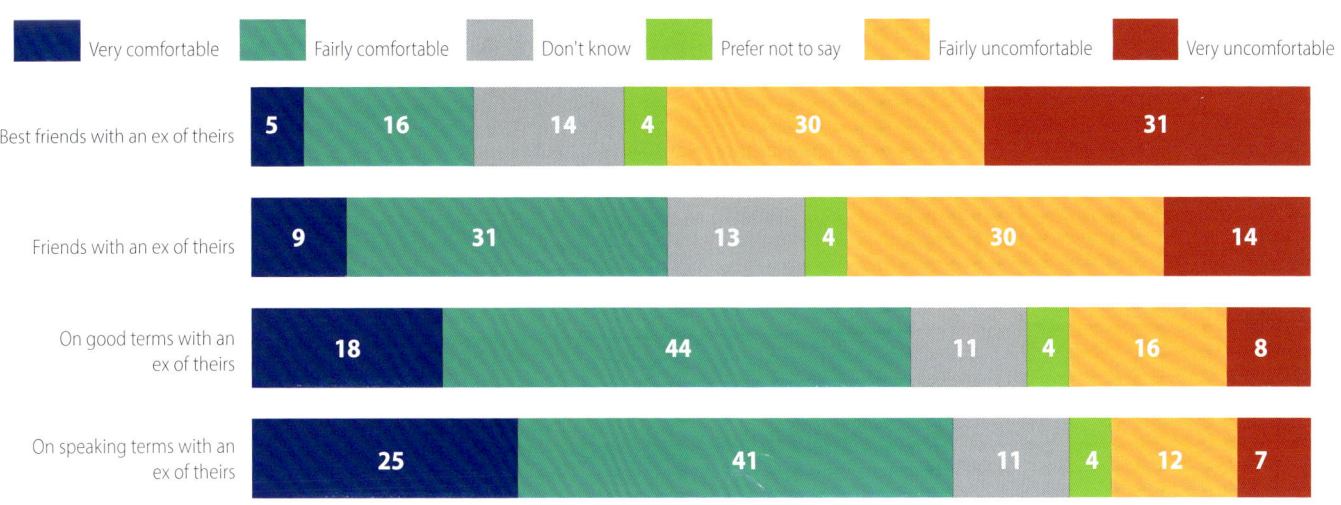

relationship, with three in 10 (31%) saying they would prefer not to be and 24% unsure.

However, if a partner ended a relationship with them, Britons are split – a third (36%) of those with an ex-partner would prefer to remain friends with someone who split up with them, while four in 10 (40%) would prefer not to be friends and 23% who don't know.

Would you be comfortable with a partner of yours being friends with an ex?

If someone remains friends with their ex, is there a possibility that the sparks will be rekindled? If you're in a relationship, should you be worried if your partner is close with an ex?

The majority of the British public would be comfortable with a partner of theirs being on good terms (62%) or speaking terms (66%) with an ex. However, they are split on whether they would be happy with a partner being friends with an ex (40% comfortable, 44% uncomfortable) and would not be happy with a partner of theirs being best friends with their ex (21% comfortable, 61% uncomfortable).

In general, men are more likely to say they would be comfortable than women with a partner of theirs being best friends with an ex (26% vs 17%), although this difference is not seen in friends, good terms or speaking terms. Seven in 10 (69%) women would be uncomfortable with their partner being best friends with an ex, compared to half (52%) of men.

When relationships end, what do Britons normally do – and what do they expect their friends and family to do?

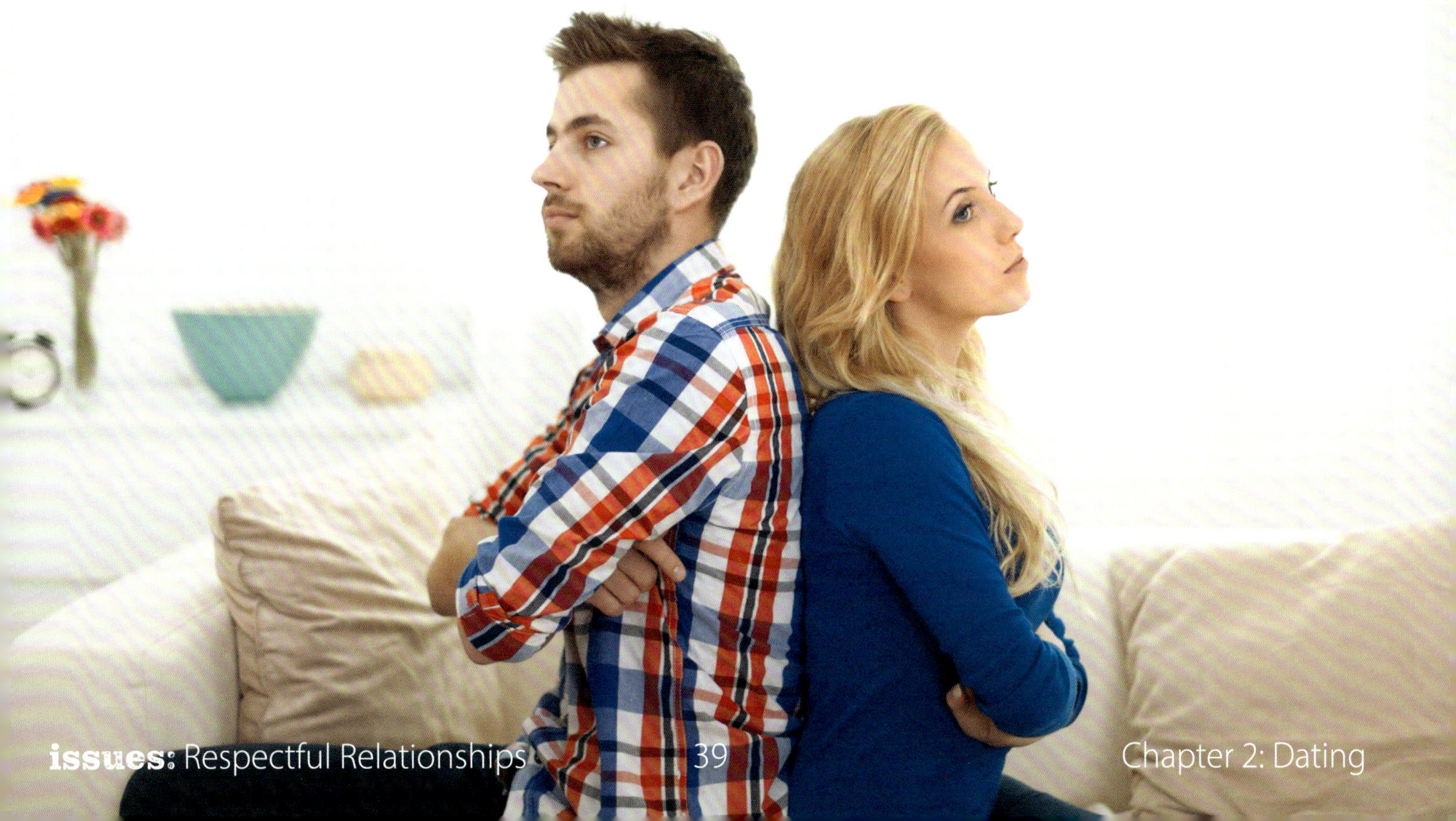

The ending of a relationship, particularly a long-term one, is not just the breaking up of two people, it represents the unwinding of two lives. Do you unfollow your ex on social media, return their possessions or otherwise purge their existence from your home, wardrobe and online presence?

More than half (57%) of Britons with an ex-partner do have some things that they would normally do following the end of a relationship. By far the most common choice after splitting up with a partner is returning any possessions of theirs (40%) – but just 6% would throw away any presents their ex bought them over the course of a relationship.

What things do Britons do at the end of a relationship?

Generally speaking, when a relationship ends, what things would you normally do straight afterwards? Please select all that apply.
% of 1344 British adults with an ex-partner

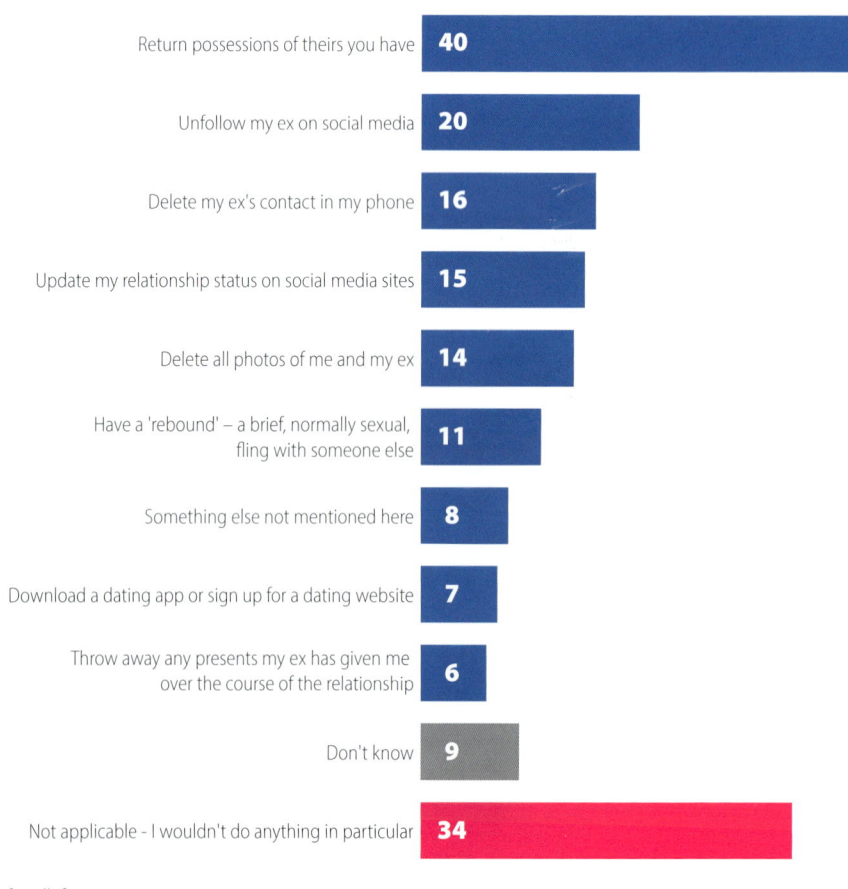

Source: YouGov

One in five (20%) Britons with an ex would unfollow their partner on social media if the relationship ended, while 16% would delete their ex's contact details in their phone, 15% would update their relationship status and 14% would delete all photos of them and their ex-partner. One in nine (11%) Britons with an ex would go on the rebound – having a brief, normally sexual, fling with someone else to get over their broken heart.

Men and women deal with relationships ending differently. Men are more likely than women to say they would have a rebound after a relationship, by 14% to 8%, while women are more likely than men to unfollow their ex on social media (24% to 16%) and return their ex's possessions (44% to 35%).

A third of Britons with an ex-partner (34%) say they wouldn't do anything in particular after a relationship ends, and most (55%) say they wouldn't have any expectations for how their friends and family should act when they go through a break-up.

Of the third (35%) who say they would expect their friends and family to change their behaviour after they go through a breakup, by far the most common choice was a quarter (25%) of those with an ex-partner saying they would expect their friends and family not to spend time with their ex. In addition, 15% would expect their loved ones not to speak to their ex-partner any more and 13% say their family and friends should return any of their ex's possessions.

A digital age requires a digital breakup, and if your friends and family follow your ex on social media, it's possible that you might be subject to unwelcome updates from their life without you. However, just one in 10 (10%) of Britons with an ex-partner would expect their nearest and dearest to unfollow their ex on social media.

Hostile break-ups: how should you act around the ex-partner of a close friend

When a relationship ends, what things do Britons expect their friends and family to do?

Generally speaking, when a relationship ends, what things would you expect your friends and family to do? Please select all that apply.
% of 1344 British adults with an ex-partner

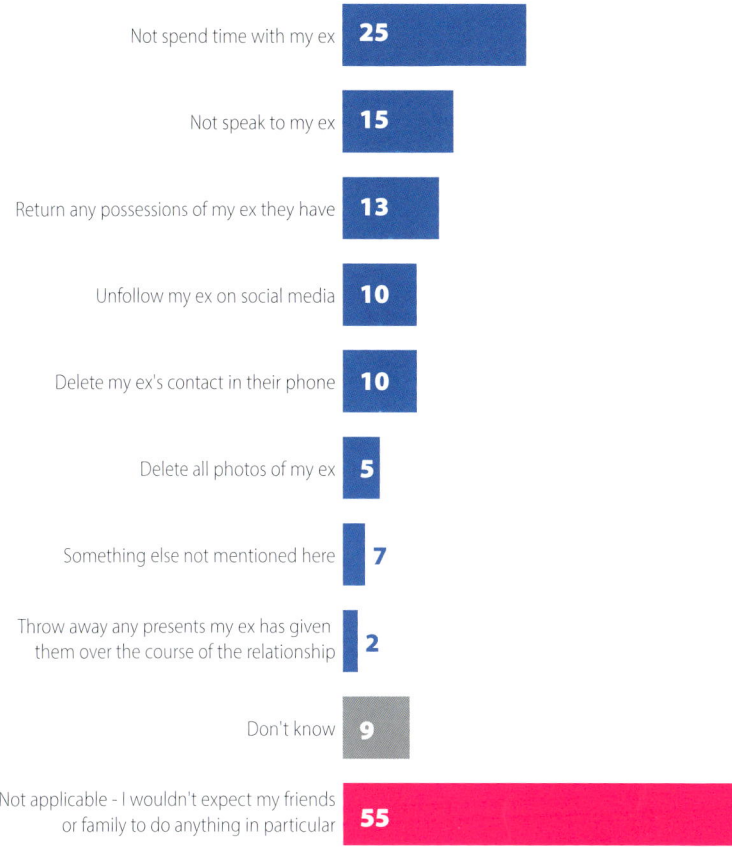

- Not spend time with my ex: 25
- Not speak to my ex: 15
- Return any possessions of my ex they have: 13
- Unfollow my ex on social media: 10
- Delete my ex's contact in their phone: 10
- Delete all photos of my ex: 5
- Something else not mentioned here: 7
- Throw away any presents my ex has given them over the course of the relationship: 2
- Don't know: 9
- Not applicable - I wouldn't expect my friends or family to do anything in particular: 55

Source: YouGov

or family member, if the breakup was unfriendly?

How would you act if you saw the former partner of a close friend, or family member, and you knew they'd had an acrimonious break-up? Does loyalty compel you to be unfriendly to that person?

British politeness wins out in this case, it appears. Two-thirds of the British public (64%) would be civil, but not friendly, to the former partner of someone close to them if the break-up between those two people was a hostile one. One in 10 (10%) would be friendly, and just 7% would be openly unfriendly.

The numbers are almost identical for how Britons would expect their friends and family to act if they ran into someone with whom they'd had a hostile break-up, with 61% expecting civility, but not friendliness, 11% saying they would want their loved ones to be friendly to their ex and 7% unfriendly.

21 February 2022

The majority of Britons would expect their friends and family to be civil to someone they had a hostile break up with

For each of the following scenarios, please select the answer that most applies... %

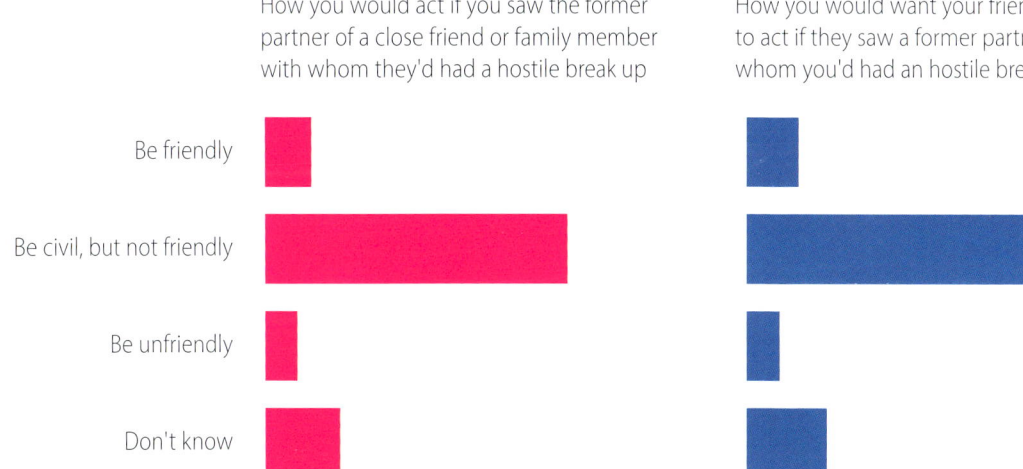

	How you would act if you saw the former partner of a close friend or family member with whom they'd had a hostile break up	How you would want your friends and family to act if they saw a former partner of yours with whom you'd had an hostile break up
Be friendly		
Be civil, but not friendly		
Be unfriendly		
Don't know		

Source: YouGov

The above information is reprinted with kind permission from YouGov.
© 2023 YouGov PLC

www.yougov.co.uk

Useful Websites/ Where can I find help

Useful Websites

www.brook.org.uk

www.counselling-directory.org.uk

www.ditchthelabel.org

www.exposure.org.uk

www.healthforteens.co.uk

www.hiddenstrength.com

www.independent.co.uk

www.metro.co.uk

www.positive.news

www.psychreg.org

www.relate.org.uk

www.revealedprojects.org.uk

www.surrey.ac.uk

www.teenagehelpline.org.uk

www.theethicalist.com

www.theguardian.com

www.thinkyouknow.co.uk

www.yes-shecan.com

www.yougov.co.uk

www.youthemployment.org.uk

www.youthscape.co.uk

Where can I find help?

Below are some telephone numbers, email addresses and websites of agencies or charities that can offer support or advice if you, or someone you know needs it.

Brook
You can contact an advisor by text on 07717 989 023 (standard SMS rates).
www.brook.org.uk

ChildLine
Helpline: 0800 11 11
www.childline.org.uk

Child Exploitation and Online Protection Centre (CEOP)
www.ceop.police.uk

The Mix
Helpline: 0808 808 4994
www.themix.org.uk

Thinkuknow
www.thinkuknow.co.uk

Glossary

Adolescent
A young person – someone in a transitional phase between child and adult.

Baiting
A method of provocation. To intentionally make someone angry by doing or saying things to annoy them.

Banter
An exchange of teasing remarks.

Bullying
A form of aggressive behaviour used to intimidate someone. It can be inflected both physically and mentally (psychologically).

Catfishing
A type of impersonation involving stealing someone's identity and posing as them to deceive others.

CEOP
Child Exploitation and Online Protection – CEOP is a law enforcement agency and is there to help keep children and young people safe from sexual abuse and grooming online.

Consent
The act of giving permission for something to happen. This can include medical consent, such as giving permission for a medical procedure to be carried out, or sexual consent – to give permission to a partner to take part in a sexual act.

Cyberbullying
Cyberbullying is when technology is used to harass, embarrass or threaten to hurt someone. A lot is done through social networking sites such as Facebook and Twitter. Bullying via mobile phones is also a form of cyberbullying. With the use of technology on the rise, there are more and more incidents of cyberbullying.

Digital abuse
Most frequently occurring in teenage relationships, digital abuse involves the use of texting and social networking sites to keep track of, harass, stalk, control, bully or intimidate a partner.

Domestic abuse
Any incident of physical, sexual, emotional or financial abuse that takes place within an intimate partner relationship. Domestic abuse can be perpetrated by a spouse, partner or other family member and occurs regardless of gender, sex, race, class or religion.

Emotional abuse
Emotional abuse refers to a victim being verbally attacked, criticised and put down. Following frequent exposure to this abuse, the victim's mental wellbeing suffers as their self-esteem is destroyed and the perpetrator's control over them increases. They may suffer from feelings of worthlessness, believing that they deserve the abuse or that if they were to leave the abuser they would never find another partner. A victim may also have been convinced by their abuser that the abuse is their fault. The abuser can use these feelings to manipulate the victim.

Grooming
Actions that are deliberately performed in order to encourage a child to engage in sexual activity. For example, offering friendship and establishing an emotional connection, buying gifts, etc.

Harassment
Usually persistent (but not always), a behaviour that is intended to cause distress and offence. It can occur on the school playground, in the workplace and even at home.

Loneliness
A feeling of being alone and isolated. Often those without social contact will feel lonely, but it is possible to feel lonely even when surrounded by others.

Rape
Forcing someone to engage in sexual intercourse against their will. Force is not necessarily physical, it could also be emotional or psychological.

Revenge porn
Revenge porn refers to distributing or making public explicit images or videos of a former partner.

Safe sex
Being safe with sex means caring for both your own health, and the health of your partner. Being safe protects you from getting or passing on STIs and from unplanned pregnancy.

Sexting
Someone uploading and sending an indecent, usually sexually graphic, image to their friend or boy/girlfriend via mobile phone or the Internet.

Sexual abuse
Sexual abuse occurs when a victim is forced into a sexual act against their will, through violence or intimidation. This can include rape. Sexual abuse is always a crime, no matter what the relationship is between the victim and perpetrator.

Sexual bullying
This includes a range of behaviours such as sexualised name-calling and verbal abuse, mocking someone's sexual performance, ridiculing physical appearance, criticising sexual behaviour, spreading rumours about someone's sexuality or about sexual experiences they have had or not had, unwanted touching and physical assault. Sexual bullying is behaviour which is repeated over time and intends to victimise someone by using their gender, sexuality or sexual (in)experience to hurt them.

Index

A
alcohol, and consent 31

B
baiting 43
break-ups
    dating 21, 36–41
    friendships 5, 12–15
bullying 13, 43

C
capacity, and consent 31
catfishing 43
child sex offences 26
coercion 31
communication 1, 20, 22, 25
compromise 20
consent 20, 25–27, 30–35
    legal age of 31
    withdrawing 31–32
controlling behaviour 22
cyberbullying 43

D
dating
    break-ups 21, 36–41
    consent 20, 25–27, 30-35
    first love 16–17
    healthy relationships 20–21, 24
    infatuation 18
    red flags 22–23
    sex 24–26, 31
    sexting 27–29
    unsafe relationships 21
digital abuse 43
domestic abuse 32, 43
dopamine 16, 18–19

E
emotional abuse 21, 22, 43
ex-partners 22, 38–41

F
first love 16–17
forgiveness 1
frenemies 6–7
friendships
    break-ups 5, 12–15
    consent 30
    frenemies 6–7
    intergenerational 10–11
    making friends 8–9
    negative 3–7
    positive 1–3
    toxic 3

G
gaslighting 22
ghosting 13, 36
Good Lad Initiative (GLI) 34
grooming 43
gut feelings 22

H
harassment 43
    see also sexual harassment
healthy relationships 20–21, 24
honesty 1, 17, 20, 36

I
individuality 20
infatuation 18–19
intergenerational friendships 10–11
introverts 9

J
jealousy 22

K
kindness 1, 24

L
loneliness 10, 43
love
    falling in love 18–19
    first love 16–17
    what love is 17–19
    see also dating
love-bombing 22

M
messages, sexual 27–29

N
norepinephrine 16
nude photos *see* sexting

O
oxytocin 16, 18–19

P
pornography 27

R
rape 25, 26, 31, 32, 43
red flags 22–23

Relationships, Sex, and Health Education (RHSE) 33, 35
respect 1, 20–21

S
safe sex 25, 43
serotonin 16
sex 24–27, 31
    see also consent
sexting 27–29, 43
sexual abuse 26–27, 33, 43
sexual activity 26, 31
sexual assault 26, 31
sexual bullying 43
sexual harassment 26, 31
Sexual Offences Act 2003 31
sexual violence 31–33

T
toxic friendships 3
trust 1, 20

U
unsafe relationships 21